"Kyra? Tell me what you want."

The stranger's breath was hot against her ear. And oh, did she want him! The feeling whipped through her like a hurricane—wild, untamed and very, very tempting.

Kyra had purchased a fantasy vacation that she'd assumed she could leave behind. A week of hedonism and then things would be back to normal. This longing in her gut would be out of her system. And she'd go back to her fiancé and the rest of her life.

Was she a fool to think she could just walk away? Kyra gnawed on her lip, not at all sure that hedonism was her thing after all. Drawing a fortifying breath, she reached up to capture his hand in hers. "I should go."

She started to back away, but before she could put any distance between them, the stranger moved forward. In one bold, possessive move, he gripped her arms, gently but firmly. Kyra's breath quickened as he closed the distance between them. She had to put a stop to this right now. It would lead her someplace dangerous. Dangerous for her heart. Confusing for her mind.

She needed to walk away...but heaven help her, she couldn't. When his mouth closed over hers, Kyra could only moan as her body melted into his....

Dear Reader,

What would you do if you discovered a place where your every fantasy could be indulged, where sensuality you've only dreamed about could become reality? Well, welcome to Intimate Fantasy, an island paradise designed to satisfy every erotic craving.

Kyra Cartright is looking to experience everything— life, love, *incredible sex*—before she returns home to throw herself into the family business and a marriage of convenience. An anonymous fling with a dark sexy stranger by night seems to be just what she needs. But she realizes that falling for shy, sexy Tony Moretti during the days can be very satisfying, too! How can she choose between the two men? Well, maybe she doesn't have to....

I hope you enjoy *Intimate Fantasy* and the rest of the books in the FANTASIES INC. miniseries. And be sure to look for my first Harlequin BLAZE title, *L.A. Confidential,* available in November. In the meantime, I'd love to hear from you. You can write to me at P.O. Box 151417, Austin, TX 78715-1417 (send a SASE if you'd like some goodies!) or check out my Web site at www.juliekenner.com.

Happy Reading,

Julie Kenner

Books by Julie Kenner

HARLEQUIN TEMPTATION
772—NOBODY DOES IT BETTER
801—RECKLESS

INTIMATE
FANTASY
Julie Kenner

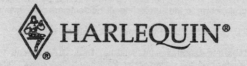

TORONTO • NEW YORK • LONDON
AMSTERDAM • PARIS • SYDNEY • HAMBURG
STOCKHOLM • ATHENS • TOKYO • MILAN • MADRID
PRAGUE • WARSAW • BUDAPEST • AUCKLAND

Thanks to all the folks who helped me with the details.
For helping me with the flying lingo, Susan Grant and my dad, Charles Beck (who, years ago, actually let me take the controls of his Cessna—even before I was old enough to see out the window!). And thanks to Jane Mick, Myrna Ward and Julie Ortolon for the wonderful help with the sailing terminology, possibilities and problems. Your input was invaluable, but any errors are my own. Also, thanks to Dr. John Pearce, who fixed my wrist so that I could type this book. And of course, thanks to Janelle and Karen....
I've had a blast!

And finally, thanks to little Kyra Tomlin,
for letting me borrow her name.

ISBN 0-373-25940-9

INTIMATE FANTASY

____Prologue____

CHARLIE "C.J." MILLER cast a sidelong glance toward his dozing passenger. The poor girl had been awake for over thirty-six hours, thanks to thunderstorms in Texas and cancelled flights. Though she'd made polite small talk before they took off, she'd finally curled up against the pillow he'd offered, clutching a spiral notebook in her lap.

Despite being new to the job, C.J. had already transported a dozen or so people from the Miami dock to one of the four lush island resorts that made up Fantasies, Inc.—Wild Fantasy, Seductive Fantasy, Secret Fantasy, and today's destination, Intimate Fantasy. His current passenger, Kyra Cartwright, was girl-next-door pretty, about the age of his oldest daughter, with sandy brown hair that fell in soft waves over her cheeks. Her lips were parted in sleep, as if she didn't have a care in the world.

C.J. knew better, of course. Fantasies, Inc. existed for one purpose only—to make people's dreams, wishes and longings come true. And a young woman with a yearning strong enough to send her to one of the islands definitely had a care or two.

As the resort's only pilot, C.J. was privy to enough information about each guest's fantasy to ensure that he didn't accidentally say the wrong thing or make the guest uncomfortable. The portion of Ms. Cartwright's application that he'd seen had put a smile on his face. She'd typed a thesis sentence—*Why would a successful career girl from one of radio's first families want to spend a week chasing adventure on a sun-splashed island?*—and then carefully outlined her reasons. Below that, in descending order from most to least appealing, she'd laid out the types of adventures she had in mind.

Although the outline resembled a business plan, as a whole, the application was anything but dry and corporate. In her neatly typed list, Kyra Cartwright had bared her soul, explaining how she intended to save her family's business by accepting her boyfriend's marriage proposal. But instead of feeling excited or nervous or any of a dozen other bride-like emotions, she simply felt lost.

That conclusion had been followed by a list of possible reasons, along with adventurous—even sensual—solutions. C.J. knew exactly where she was coming from. She wanted to rid herself of that antsy feeling in her gut, needed to silence the little voice in her head that kept asking: *Hey, kid, this is the rest of your life we're talking about. Are you sure you know what you're doing? Shouldn't you maybe step out a bit and take a look around?*

During his own youth that voice had taunted C.J., too. But unlike his passenger, he'd had no choice. The

Vietnam War had called, and he'd had to go. After that...well, his path had been pretty much set.

Ms. Cartwright, at least, had Fantasies, Inc.

The owner, Merrilee Schaefer-Weston, handpicked each guest from detailed applications describing the desired fantasy. In Ms. Cartwright's case, C.J. couldn't help but wonder how much of a role Merrilee's own comfortable but passionless marriage had played in her decision to offer the young woman a tantalizing week on Intimate Fantasy.

As always, when he thought about Merrilee and their years apart, a wave of melancholy washed over him, bittersweet memories laced with fresh, new desire. Frustrated, he rubbed his aching neck and concentrated only on flying. With a light touch, he banked the resort's sturdy Cessna 206 seaplane, correcting its course. He glanced at the fuel gauge and the altimeter, drawing reassurance from the familiar controls and the easy way the plane responded.

Life never responded that well. Certainly his—and Merrilee's—had taken an unexpected turn. As much as he'd loved his wife, and as much as he'd mourned her death two years ago, the simple fact remained that Merrilee had been his first, best love. But no yoke, no rudder, no ailerons could have kept their love on course when the war had intervened. Fate had stepped in, and there hadn't been a damn thing he could do about it.

Damn, but he'd wanted so much more for her—*for*

them. And it was small comfort knowing that Oliver Weston had provided well for the woman who should have been C.J.'s. Upon Weston's death, Merrilee had inherited millions, and she'd poured her passion into Fantasies, Inc. Now, it seemed, Merrilee thrived on bringing happiness to others.

Soon, C.J. hoped, he'd be able to bring some new joy to her as well. Lord knew, she deserved it.

"Intimate Base to Alpha-Victor-Oh-Oh-Niner, do you copy? C.J., where the devil are you?"

The voice rang in his headset, and he pushed the mike closer so he could respond without waking Ms. Cartwright. "Roger, I copy. I'm approaching from the east."

"Roger that," Chris said from the office on Intimate Fantasy.

C.J. peered down at the cluster of lush islands that made up the Fantasies, Inc. resort, then spotted the lagoon at Intimate Fantasy. "Got the landing area in sight."

"You're clear to land at your discretion."

"Roger." He cleared his throat. "Is Ms. Weston planning to meet the plane?"

A burst of static filled his ear.

"Say again?"

"Not sure," Chris said, enunciating clearly. "Last I heard, she got held up on Wild Fantasy, but she's hoping to make it."

"Copy and out." C.J. sighed, pulling the headphones

off, wishing he knew for certain if he'd be seeing her today. So far, he'd only glimpsed her from afar. Up close, would she recognize him? He didn't think so. His face was weathered, the ravages of both time and the war having taken their toll, and his once-black hair was now salt-and-pepper. Hopefully, she wouldn't recognize him until he was ready. Just in case, he'd taken the added precaution of growing a moustache. And his reflective aviator sunglasses and battered Air Force cap didn't hurt either.

Plus, she'd known him only as Charlie. He hadn't been christened with his current nickname until the war. So as far as Merrilee knew, C.J. Miller was a complete stranger...at least for a little while longer.

Glancing down, he searched the blue water below, trying without success to see Merrilee's small boat darting between the islands. Even after almost forty years in a cockpit, it still amazed him how tranquil the world looked from the air. Of course, the Florida Keys tended to look peaceful even from the ground, but there was something magical about the way the vibrant green islands burst out of the crystal blue ocean.

He chuckled. He was getting sentimental in his old age. Very sentimental, actually. Hadn't he signed on as Fantasies, Inc.'s new pilot in order to be close to Merrilee? To see if, after all these years, they could rekindle their love for each other?

Crazy old fool. There was no rekindling needed on his end. The love he'd felt for Merrilee all those years ago hadn't faded one iota over the passing decades. And now, what he wanted more than anything was to run to her. To hold her in his arms and make the years melt away. But he also needed to be sure. The last thing in the world he wanted was to make Merrilee uncomfortable. No, he'd inadvertently caused her too much grief already.

He suppressed a shudder, holding the small plane steady as the memories haunted him, the wail of bullets and the screams of his buddies echoing through his mind. When his fighter had been shot down, he'd done what he had to do to survive. Wounded, he'd crawled through the mire until he'd come across the body of an officer whose life had already slipped away.

With a silent prayer, C.J. had exchanged his own dog tags—which clearly identified him as an enlisted man—for the officer's. The N.V.A. often shot enlisted men on sight, but officers were kept alive for interrogation. As he'd hoped, the trick had saved his life, and not a day went by that C.J. didn't thank the man for sharing his name.

As if being a prisoner of war hadn't been terrible enough, the real horror had been coming home to discover his worst fear realized—that Merrilee, believing him dead, had married one of her father's colleagues. And even though he'd eventually married a fine woman, and though he'd loved Evelyn with all his heart, C.J. had never stopped loving Merrilee, had never stopped thinking about her.

It wasn't until too late that he'd learned through the grapevine that Merrilee's marriage was a loveless one. When he'd first returned from Nam, he couldn't bring himself to interfere with what he assumed was a happy, healthy marriage. He certainly hadn't wanted to put himself between her and her new husband. It had seemed easier on both of them—and fairer to her—to simply let her believe he'd been killed during the war. And later, when C.J. gleaned the truth about Merrilee's relationship with Weston, he had Evelyn and his girls.

About a year after he lost Evelyn to cancer, he'd thought about finding Merrilee. But by then, he'd lost track.

A few months later, he'd read about her successful resort in the Florida Keys, and the next thing he knew, he'd signed on as the company pilot.

You are a crazy old fool. He grinned. Maybe he was. But he intended to give this his best shot, to make it up to her. He wanted Merrilee to know she was still special and loved—and always had been.

In the right-hand seat, his passenger shifted, her eyes fluttering open.

"Welcome back," he said. "How are you feeling, Ms. Cartwright?"

She smiled. "Kyra, please. And I'm much better, Mr...."

"Miller," he said, reminding her. "C. J. Miller."

She shifted her arm, revealing the notebook on her

lap. He caught a glimpse of a few neatly printed items running down the page, each one with a checkmark beside it: plane ticket, cab fare, tip for bellboy, magazine for plane, undies and makeup in carry-on.

He glanced out the side window to hide his grin, deciding that more and more she reminded him of his daughter. When he turned back, she seemed a little less nervous than before.

She looked up at him, her gray eyes wide. "I still can't believe we're just going to land on the water."

"Believe me, ma'am, in this type of plane, you don't want me bringing it down on land."

"Well, I did come to Fantasies, Inc. for an adventure." Her laugh was warm and cheerful, but the way she twisted her hands in her lap suggested that she was simply doing a good job of hiding her nerves.

"I promise I know what I'm doing."

She glanced down, sheepish, and untangled her hands. "Sorry. It's not...I mean, it's true I'm not crazy about small planes, but..." She trailed off, rolling one shoulder in a half-shrug.

He grinned. "But that's not all you're nervous about."

Her hesitant smile was answer enough. "I guess you see a lot of this," she said. "Guests, that is, scared silly of their own fantasy."

"Not too many. Nervous, yes, I've seen a lot of that." He turned to face her. "Are you? Scared, I mean."

She pondered the question. "No, I suppose not. Not

really. Not about this, anyway." She looked down at the hands she was again twisting in her lap. "I've made up my mind to get married soon, and I suppose I'm a little nervous about that. But I've gone over all the pros and cons." She clutched the spiral notebook to her chest. "I'm sure I'm doing the right thing. But I guess I still need a week alone before I do it."

"That makes perfect sense to me."

"Really?"

He nodded. "Absolutely."

"Thanks." She smiled, almost shyly. "I have to admit, I'm terribly curious as to how everything is going to come together. But I trust Ms. Weston."

He nodded, trying to convey a wealth of understanding and support in his simple gesture. "You should. Merrilee would never steer you wrong."

This time her smile was grateful. "I could tell that about her right off." She frowned, as if trying to decide whether or not to say more. "I told my dad and my brother that I was going to a business conference. Sometimes I wonder what they'd say if they knew I was vacationing at a fantasy resort. I suppose they'd think I'm being silly and self-indulgent."

He wanted to tell her that the one thing she needed to do was follow her heart. Instead, he simply smiled. "No, not silly at all. I think you're being honest." He reached over and patted her hand. "If you were my daughter I'd be proud. It takes a lot of guts to realize there may be other paths our lives can take. There's nothing selfish about wanting to rack up a few experiences before moving on to the next phase of your life."

"Thank you," she said, her words almost a sigh.

"You're welcome. And thanks for keeping me company during the flight."

"Some company." She laughed, her cheeks flushing. "Unless I talk in my sleep."

He matched her laugh, then nodded out the window at the water rising up to meet them. "Ready?"

She raised her eyebrows. "Do I have a choice?"

"Not unless you feel like parachuting."

"Then by all means, Mr. Miller, take us down."

Water landings were always choppy, but this one was smoother than most, and C.J. congratulated himself for not shaking Kyra up any more than necessary. He taxied to the dock, then killed the engine as the staff moored the plane and opened Kyra's door. C.J. slid out of his seat and climbed into the back of the plane, gathering her luggage and passing it out the back door to Stuart, one of the college kids who did odd jobs during the summer months.

Ducking to keep from whacking his head on the doorframe, he climbed out of the plane, careful not to slip on the wet dock. When he stood up, there she was.

His Merrilee. Standing right there in front of him. Just as beautiful, just as vibrant, as he'd remembered her. Over the past few weeks, he'd seen her, sure. But not this close, so close he could almost smell her perfume. White Shoulders. For decades, his eyes had scoured the room whenever he caught that scent, but never once had he found Merrilee. Until now.

He realized she was smiling at him, one hand held out for him to take. He grasped hers firmly, glad for the glasses and cap, wondering if she had even an inkling as to who he really was.

"It's a pleasure to finally meet you," she said, the curl of her fingers over his wreaking havoc with his head. "I've been trying to come by and welcome you to the Fantasies family, but we seem to keep missing each other."

"Fancy that," he mumbled.

"Yes. Well..." She took her hand back, then cocked her head slightly, her eyes lingering on him before she finally blinked. "At any rate, please come by the office later and let's schedule a time to talk. I like to take every employee through an orientation, and you're long past due."

"Of course," he said, intending no such thing.

Her smile was a little shaky, but when she turned to Kyra, her professional demeanor was back in place. "I'm sure you're going to enjoy your stay."

"I know I will," Kyra said. She nodded toward C.J. "And thanks again, Mr. Miller. I especially appreciated the landing."

With a grin, he tapped the brim of his cap, his finger hesitating there when he noticed the puzzled expression on Merrilee's face.

"Ma'am?"

Her cheeks flushed. "I'm sorry. It's nothing. You just...you remind me of someone. But, no, that's silly. It's not..." She trailed off, then shook herself, standing straighter as C.J. marveled at the poised, confident woman she'd become. "Never mind," she said and took Kyra's arm. "Stuart will take you to your cabin. After you're settled, we'll have dinner and I'll give you a brief orientation."

C.J. watched Merrilee guide the younger woman down the dock toward the waiting Jeep, his stomach in knots. There had been a spark of recognition in her eyes, extinguished by disappointment when she remembered what she believed to be the truth—that her Charlie was lost to her forever.

He took a deep breath, trying to calm the dogfight going on in his stomach. Soon, he'd tell her the truth. And maybe, just maybe, they still had a chance to make both their fantasies come true.

1

FROM HER cabana doorway, Kyra looked out over the private beach, watching as the tropical sun reflected off the near-white sand, and the froth from the breaking waves launched tiny rainbows into the sky. The place fairly sparkled with magic, dripping with possibility and promise.

The perfect place for a fantasy.

A shiver of anticipation tingled up her spine, and she hugged herself. "This is it, kid," she whispered. "Now or never."

With a determined tug, she pulled the jacket of her favorite Anne Klein suit over her shoulders and tossed it into the corner. One quick tug on the zipper and the rest of the outfit followed, the skirt falling to the ground in a pile of fine linen.

She kicked the skirt in the direction of the jacket, knowing full well that before the hour was up, she'd have both items on hangers and in the closet. In the meantime, though, she was going to let the island work its magic, and she stood in the doorway of her isolated cabin, breathing deep, wearing nothing but a soft silk shell and panties.

Free. For one week, she had nothing but an unsure future in front of her. No Day-Timer, no appointments, no obligations.

It felt wonderful. Weird and unfamiliar, but wonderful.

A fresh wave of guilt crested in her gut, but she firmly quashed it. She deserved this. For the last sixteen years, she'd lived her life for her father and brother, holding the family together, being the rock, just as she'd promised her mother when the cancer had made it only too clear that Kyra was soon to be the sole female in the Cartwright household.

A heck of a lot for a ten-year-old to shoulder, but she'd never once complained. Not when she'd taken over the chores instead of playing with the neighborhood kids. Not when her father's failing health had forced her to sacrifice her college social life so that she could help him with the day-to-day operations of Cartwright Radio. Not even when she'd given up her own chance at an M.B.A. so that her brother, Evan, could go to medical school.

She adored her father and brother, and she loved everything about working in radio. And for those simple reasons, her choices had never seemed like sacrifices.

Now, though...

Her father's health had worsened, and Kyra's world was on shaky ground. For over thirty years, Milton Cartwright had been the backbone of their family-owned chain of radio stations, his own syndicated show the company's cash cow. Almost everyone in the country tuned in for Milton's peculiar brand of Texas humor mixed with a dash of Dallas sophistication.

What most folks didn't realize was just how poorly the radio guru had been getting on these past few years. Now everything her father had struggled for was threatened. The moment Milton retired and his show went off the air, the advertising dollars would dry up. And that meant the family business would be dead and gone.

Of course, Milton Cartwright knew that as well as all the vultures circling the station's offices in downtown Dallas. To Kyra's infinite frustration, her dad was determined not to give them the satisfaction. He was going to stay on the radio until the last possible second.

As much as she wanted the business to survive, Kyra was more determined to make sure her dad stayed as healthy as possible for as long as possible. According to his cadre of doctors, that meant early retirement. But the man was as stubborn as they came, and unless Kyra found some way to ensure the station would continue to bring in key advertisers, he wasn't about to turn over the reins of the company to anyone.

After months of pounding her head against the wall, Kyra'd been on the verge of conceding defeat when she found her answer—a good luck charm in a pinstripe suit. Harold Stovall, President and Chairman of United Media Corporation. A longtime friend, he'd recently promised to let Cartwright Radio acquire not one but two of his key on-air personalities.

And, really, he hadn't asked that much in return. After all, the business meant everything to Kyra's father, and Milton Cartwright meant everything to Kyra.

She held on to the doorjamb, feeling her body go rigid as the knowledge of what lay ahead settled into her bones. Truly, Harold was a dear, and fifteen years wasn't that big an age difference. They'd even dated for a while, back when Kyra had lived in New York while she learned the ropes of working at a major radio station.

So what if he'd never made her toes tingle or her knees go weak? He'd always been kind and gentle. And he truly adored her.

Most important, she knew with absolute certainty that he'd protect her father's business as if it were his own, something Kyra couldn't do alone. Without Harold, Kyra would lose everything.

In a way, Harold was giving her the world. It was only fair that she give him herself in return.

So she'd decided to agree. After this trip, she'd tell him, and in just a few months, she would become Mrs. Harold Stovall. She'd give herself over to a marriage based on respect, if not love.

She'd always thrown herself into her work. Now, her work would be her life.

Except there was still that one, traitorous little part of her. An unsatisfied, rebellious, needy part of her. She hated to even let it in, hated to admit she didn't have the strength to ignore the piece of her that longed for...she wasn't sure what.

Her best friend, Mona, had said that Kyra was coming to Intimate Fantasy to sow her wild oats, but that wasn't it. Not exactly. She'd lived her entire life in a cocoon. A warm and loving cocoon, true, but that didn't make the binds any less tight.

Her whole life, she'd done the right thing, been the good girl. And her future promised to be exactly the same. But for one week, Kyra wanted to see what else the world offered.

For twenty-six years, she'd been living a perfectly ordered existence doing what everyone expected. But here, now...she wanted the whole enchilada. Wanted to take a running leap off a cliff and fly out into life.

She would marry Harold, yes. And, once spoken, she would honor her wedding vows.

But here...now...

Now, she was at a fantasy resort. She'd cashed in the savings bonds her mother had left her, emptied her meager savings account, and come here for the fantasy of a lifetime. Not responsible, not reasonable, but something she had to do.

With a sigh, she ran her fingers through her hair. Right now, she wanted passion. Weak-kneed, heart-pounding, scream-inducing passion. And not just sex, but a passion for life. She wanted to feel the blood pulsing in her veins. Wanted a week of adventures—sun, sea and sex. An entire week to really experience being alive.

That was her fantasy. And she wanted it so badly she could taste it. So desperately, she sometimes cried herself to sleep.

She blinked back an unexpected tear, frustrated that her control could slip so easily. A balmy breeze drifted in from the water's edge, caressing her bare arms, evaporating the tiny beads of sweat on her collarbone. With a light finger, she traced the swell of her breast under the designer silk shell. Her impractical city-girl clothes would be the first to go.

With a jerk, she grabbed the hem and yanked the shirt over her head. She tossed it in the corner with the rest of her suit, then unclipped her bra.

"Chic-a-boom, chic-a-boom, chic-a-boom, boom, boom!" She twirled it above her head and then, with one final jut of her hip, she let it sail across the room, where it landed on top of a pink lamp with a conch-shell base.

Delighted, she laughed out loud, then realized she was standing almost naked in a doorway for all the world to see.

She stepped behind the wall and poked her head outside, trying to decide if the beach was as secluded as Ms. Weston had promised. Not a soul in sight, and not a sound except for the rhythmic lap of waves against the sand.

"Kyra," she whispered, "it's time to put your money where your mouth is."

She slipped her finger under the elastic of her panties, wiggled a bit, and let them drop to the ground. Then she stepped out of her sandals and tried to judge the distance from her doorway to the ocean, bouncing on the balls of her feet as she worked up her nerve.

On the pro side, these kind of wild excursions were exactly what she was on the island for: adventure, unpredictability, thrills. On the con side, she'd be royally embarrassed if anybody saw her.

On the pro side, the water would feel wonderful. On the con side, she had no idea if the Florida waters were home to jellyfish.

On the pro side, Stuart had pointed out the cabana's first aid kit. On the con side—

"Just do it already!" Before she could stop herself, she tore out of the cabana at a full run, buck naked, sprinted across the dunes, then ran straight into the ocean. The water felt glorious against her skin, and she waded out further, finally treading water when it became too deep for her to stand.

She stayed like that for a while, enjoying the decadent sensation of the water against naked flesh. She leaned her head back, soaking her hair as she listened to the rhythm of the ocean, her mind drifting. She ought to find a giant shell for a souvenir. Then, whenever she wanted, she could press it to her ear and remember this week.

Eyes closed, she moved her arms in slow, languid movements. Just enough to keep afloat. The beach was silent. She was alone and free. Just her and nature.

Nature? She opened her eyes, looking down into the clear water to her feet and the grayish-blue blur beyond that. Was that the ocean floor? Or something else? With a sudden blinding memory, she recalled the opening scene of *Jaws*. A girl, naked, in the ocean. A shark. One heck of a creepy theme song.

Faster than she would have thought possible, she half-swam, half-ran back to the shallows, then climbed out of the water and collapsed onto the beach, inhaling gulps of air.

That was so *not* the kind of adrenaline rush she'd planned on. Closing her eyes, she let the warm sun go to work drying her wet skin. There was no one else around. No reason she couldn't lie there and enjoy the afternoon.

She bit back a self-satisfied smile. Yesterday she would never have been caught dead skinny-dipping. And lying in the sand—getting all those itchy grains all over her—well, she'd end up tracking the stuff all over the cabana.

Very messy. Very impractical.

Stifling a laugh, she picked up a handful of sand and dribbled it on her belly. For years, she'd been the responsible one—good, old, dependable Kyra.

Not anymore.

Over the next week, she was going to wear impractical clothes and let her long hair tangle in the ocean breeze. She was going to play in the surf and wear revealing bathing suits and drink fruity bar drinks with exotic names. She'd sleep until noon and dance with strangers and let someone else shoulder all the burdens for a while.

But most importantly, she was going to have adventures. Sailing. Windsurfing. Maybe even searching for sunken treasure.

And sex.

The chance to finally, *fully,* experience primitive, hot, wild sex. To succumb to a man's erotic touch. To feel that sensual trill as his fingers stroked and played her. That, perhaps, was the biggest adventure of all.

She was going to do all that and more, and she didn't feel even a tiny bit selfish. Well, maybe a little, but she was working really hard to quash the feeling. This was her fantasy, after all. She'd come to this island to lose herself…and, hopefully, to find herself, too.

She'd told Ms. Weston she wanted the sun, the sea and sex. If that combination didn't make her feel alive, then nothing would.

Next week, when her fantasy was over, she'd return to Dallas—to Harold, and to her obligations. But this week… This week, she was going to make enough memories to last her the rest of her life.

THE JEEP bounced along the uneven terrain, and Kyra grabbed on to the roll bar to steady herself. After an hour-long shower to get rid of the sand, she'd changed into a sundress, and now her skirt billowed with the vehicle's motion. She'd pulled her hair back into a ponytail, but the wind had loosed a few tendrils. Now she pushed the renegade locks out of her eyes and mouth, making a mental note to buy barrettes in the gift shop.

In the driver's seat, her coconut-scented, college-aged chauffeur kept a nonchalant hand draped over the steering wheel. "It's just this one patch that's rough," Stuart said, his sun-bleached hair and deep tan making him look like he should be riding a wave instead of driving a 4x4.

He nodded toward a cluster of palm trees standing like sentries guarding the entrance of the little cove. "The road's just past those trees, and then the restaurant's less than a mile away."

"I'm fine," Kyra said, meaning it. The heady island atmosphere had worked its way into her blood, just like the sand from the beach had worked its way into every crevice of her body. Despite still feeling a little itchy, she felt vibrant and excited, and a bumpy ride wasn't about to change that.

"They haven't cut the road through to the outlying cabins." He glanced at her, the zinc oxide on his nose reflecting onto the lenses of his fluorescent orange sunglasses. "But it's safe, so don't worry."

"Worry?"

He turned toward her for just a second, then looked

quickly away, clamping both hands onto the steering wheel. "Nothing. Really. Just that a few folks have gotten lost out there until *he* found them. But so long as you're careful and stick to the path, you'll be fine. So forget I said anything, okay? It really is safe."

Kyra had no idea who *he* was, but if the awe in Stuart's voice was any indication, *he* was pretty impressive. "He who?"

His neck flushed crimson, a remarkable feat considering the depth of his tan, but he kept his mouth firmly shut.

Well, that did it. Now her curiosity was really piqued. "Come on, Stuart," she nagged in her best big-sister voice. "Tell me. You might as well. You already started."

He shook his head.

"Stuart..."

"Aw, man," he said. "I wasn't supposed to say anything."

She just stared at him, one eyebrow lifted in question.

"Okay, okay," he said, and Kyra stifled a triumphant smile. *Piece o' cake.*

He turned onto the main road, then shifted in his seat to face her. "The Avenger," he said, his voice low and serious.

O-kayyyy. That made no sense whatsoever. "What Avenger?"

He turned back, focusing on the road. "Well, that's

not actually his name, but I like to call him the Avenger 'cause he's, like, so totally cool. Here, I'll show you.'' He reached into the back seat, swerving a bit, and hauled a battered duffel bag into his lap. With one hand on the wheel and very little attention to the road, he rummaged in the bag, finally tossing a tattered sketch onto her lap.

Though obviously dashed off quickly, the sketch was quite well done. Through the use of bold strokes and subtle shading, the artist had managed to convey not just the image of a man standing in the shadows, but an aura of mystery as well.

Kyra's focus was drawn immediately to the man's face, mostly hidden by a low-slung cap and a thick evening beard. A pirate-style patch covered one eye, but despite the odd accoutrement, he had the face of a steady, serious man, with a firm jaw. From beyond the charcoal lines and smudges, the man's gaze seemed to burn into her, following like the eyes on the Mona Lisa. The kind of eyes that could see a woman's secrets. The kind of man who could fulfill her fantasies...

Her pulse beat an irregular rhythm in her throat, and she licked her lips. With a sigh, she tried to get her breathing back under control. It was dangerous to let her thoughts wander down that path—dangerous and intriguing. Never in her life had she experienced such a visceral reaction to a man. And not just a man, but simply the idea of a man. She shivered, her mind toying with the possibility that this mysterious, masked stranger was, in fact, her fantasy.

Stuart took a sharp corner, the abrupt movement pulling Kyra fully back to the present. Unnerved by the decidedly erotic direction of her thoughts, she tried to concentrate on the drawing itself, not the actual image. Certainly, the intensity of her reaction was a credit to the artist's skill, and Kyra looked up at Stuart with a new perspective. "Did you do this?"

He shrugged. "A hobby."

"You're good."

"Thanks. It turned out okay. I keep meaning to go back in with some color. Michael's got the most amazing green eyes."

"Michael?"

Stuart's smile was broad and proud. "Yeah. I was sketching the dock. He, uh, didn't see me until later, and when I asked him his name, that's what he told me." He shrugged. "Ms. Weston says I'm being silly, but I still like to call him the Masked Avenger."

She stifled a giggle, wondering how many comic books Stuart had stowed in his staff locker.

"He's totally cool. That's Maria's little nephew. Michael had just rescued him." He nodded toward the sketch.

"Oh, right." Embarrassed, Kyra realized she'd been so drawn to the enigmatic man in the sketch that she hadn't even noticed the child and woman huddled off to one side. "Rescued?"

Stuart swerved, steering around a pothole. "Yeah. Maria works in the administration building, and her sister's kid was visiting. He managed to wander away and we had everyone out looking for him, but no luck." He cocked his head indicating the photo. "Turns out Carlos had crawled into one of the small boats, and Michael got to him just as the kid was trying to stand up. The boat went over and, well..."

He sucked in a loud breath. "If my man hadn't come along, it coulda been bad."

Kyra's heart twisted. The little boy was one lucky fellow. "Who is this guy? A guest? How come he was right there? And why the patch?"

Stuart shrugged, focusing on the road in front of them. "Um...I don't have any idea. He ran off right after Maria showed up. Like I said, I was lucky to get a good look at him, much less learn his name. He never hangs around long enough to chat."

Interesting. Kyra traced a finger over the coarse paper as a chill raced up her spine. She imagined that it had been her in the capsized boat. She closed her eyes, her body tightening as she imagined his arms grasping her firmly below her breasts, his breath hot on her neck. He would have eased her back into his own boat, then bent over her, his lips nearing her skin, his eyes boring deep into her own. And then...

Oh my. She crossed her legs to quell a flood of purely sexual heat, then shifted in her seat as the Jeep bounced along. She needed to get her imagination under control. This man...this island...and suddenly her libido was in overdrive.

"Pretty wild, huh?" Stuart said.

"Very wild," she whispered. Then, determined to block the decadent images, she turned to better face him and scrambled for something mundane to discuss. "So you're just here for the summer?" she finally asked.

"Yup." He swung the 4x4 around a graceful stand of trees, then shifted gears. "I'll be a sophomore at U.C.L.A."

Kyra hid a smile. Maybe she'd been right about the surfing. "You're a long way from home."

He shrugged. "My grandparents live in Tampa, and it's a great job."

"Are you studying art?"

"Nope. Drama," he said. "I'm an actor." His blush resurfaced, amusing Kyra. If he had hopes of being a celebrity, he'd have to get over that shyness.

They cruised down a driveway lined with palm trees that were strung with paper lanterns. Though just barely twilight, the lanterns were already lit, and they glowed a faded orange against the pink and purple sky. Up ahead, a converted Spanish mission rose majestically, dwarfing the nearby trees.

"That's the restaurant," Stuart said.

"It's beautiful."

"Yeah, it's modeled after an historic landmark." He brought the Jeep to an abrupt halt, then picked up a clipboard with What's Your Fantasy? stenciled across the back. "Well, we're here. You're scheduled for dinner with Ms. Weston. The hostess can take you to her table."

A valet opened her door, and she stepped out. "Thanks, Stuart."

"Have fun," he said, then shifted gears and took off down the caliche drive.

She followed the hostess through the elegant restaurant to a secluded table set with fine china and silver. Ms. Weston smiled as Kyra approached. "Hello, dear."

"This is a beautiful place, Ms. Weston."

The older woman gestured to the chair opposite. "Please, call me Merrilee. I hope your accommodations are suitable," she added, as Kyra sat down.

"Fabulous. The cabana is wonderful, and the beach is, well, it's perfect."

"I'm so pleased you think so," Merrilee said, as the waiter silently approached and poured two glasses of red wine. "We try our best to make sure every aspect of our guest's stay is to their liking." She lifted her glass. "A toast. To fantasies."

"To fantasies," Kyra repeated. The clear tone of fine crystal sang out as they clinked glasses. Kyra took an experimental sip. "Chateau du Maurier, 1992. My favorite." And extremely hard to find.

"I know." Merrilee said, the corner of her lip curling into a smile.

Kyra took another sip, remembering just how much

Merrilee did know about her. The application had been long and detailed, and Kyra had spilled her soul for the first time in her life. To do her job right, Merrilee Schaefer-Weston needed to know her clients' deepest desires.

Right now, Merrilee knew more about Kyra than anyone in the world, including Evan and her father. Even more than Mona, and certainly more than Harold.

The thought was both unnerving and reassuring.

She took a roll from the bread basket and tore a piece off as she looked around the well-appointed room. There were only a few tables, each lit by the glow of sconces secured to the stone walls. The small number of patrons wasn't surprising, really. The island was an exclusive resort. At any one time, there weren't that many guests, and surely a good number of those chose to dine in privacy.

Across the room, Kyra saw C. J. Miller moving through the dimly lit restaurant, one of the guys she'd seen at the dock by his side. He still wore his cap, but the aviator glasses were gone. The two men were deep in conversation, but when C.J.'s eyes strayed her way, Kyra waved. He waved back, then quickly returned his attention to the clipboard the other man held.

Merrilee turned, then, seeing who Kyra had recognized, immediately faced forward again and took a long sip of wine. She still looked perfectly calm, but Kyra thought she might be a shade paler. The lighting, perhaps? Then again, Merrilee had seemed distracted at the dock when she'd introduced herself to the new pilot.

"Is something wrong?"

"That transparent, am I?" Merrilee's mouth curved into a smile, but it seemed a little sad. "No. Our new pilot just reminds me of someone. Someone I lost years ago." Instinctively, Kyra's eyes searched for C.J., but he'd already disappeared through the back exit.

"Even his last name...well, never mind." Merrilee shook her head and took a sip of water, as if determined to push the memories away. "We're here to talk about you, not to dredge up ghosts from my past."

"Of course," Kyra said. She was curious, but if Merrilee didn't want to talk about her lost love—and Kyra was sure it was just that—then she'd respect the other woman's wishes.

Merrilee cleared her throat. "Well then. You've read the materials, of course, but I like to meet personally with all new arrivals. At Fantasies, Inc., we don't provide the traditional resort vacation. I find the guests appreciate the opportunity to ask questions before their fantasy gets underway."

The memory of Michael was still fresh in her mind, a man who'd certainly struck a chord with her. He was the very epitome of adventure, a chivalrous knight determined to protect the innocent...and, perhaps, to fulfill her not-so-innocent fantasies?

She pictured him as a romantic recluse who lived by

nobody's rules but his own. A man who knew what it was like to feel alive and in control, to feel like he was moving through life instead of being pushed along by an uncontrollable current.

She felt a twinge of envy and considered asking if the mysterious man was there on a fantasy of his own. Even more important, did he play any role in the fantasy Merrilee had designed for her?

With a bit of effort, she quelled the urge. The woman had managed to find her favorite wine, for goodness sake. Kyra had no doubt about her ability to provide an equally impressive fantasy man.

But how? And who? Michael? She hoped so, but she didn't dare ask.

"Kyra?"

"I don't think I have any questions." None other than the big ones—*What's going to happen? And when?* She toyed with her salad fork. "Really."

Merrilee took a sip of wine, then put down her glass. "Forgive me for being so blunt, but I don't believe you."

Kyra's cheeks warmed. "It's just...I..." She took a deep breath. "I just wondered—"

"You want to know what's going to happen," Merrilee said gently. "What type of adventure is in store for you. And who you'll share it with."

Kyra nodded, silently admiring the polished woman across the table.

"There's only one rule here, my dear, and that is that

there are no rules." A smile touched her lips. "When one trades in fantasies, it's best not to be too pragmatic."

"I can see that," Kyra said, her curiosity piqued even more.

"I can't tell you how your fantasy will play out any more than I can tell you exactly what's in your heart. Only you can do that."

"But..." she paused, unsettled. "But the forms...all the questions...I told you so much about what I want, what I feel."

"And I assure you that all your information has been analyzed and put to good use." She pushed her bread plate aside and took Kyra's hand across the table. "Remember that this is *your* fantasy. A large part of it must come from you. I'm merely—" she cast her free hand about as if searching for a word "—the director of an improvisational drama. The framework is there, but much of the story comes from the players themselves."

Her smile was soft and reassuring, but did little to calm Kyra's nerves. "What if I miss my cue?"

Merrilee squeezed her hand gently before releasing it. "You won't."

Kyra nodded vaguely, wondering if, when she stumbled over her fantasy, she'd recognize it. Even more, after all her planning, all her worry, all her *longing*, would she actually have the courage to embrace it? To grab the life—the fantasy—that Merrilee had to offer?

The answer came, insistent and strong—yes, oh, yes.

"We've made a bargain, you and I," Merrilee said, as if reading her mind. "My part was—*is*—to set the stage."

"And my part?" Kyra asked, a nervous excitement cresting in her blood.

"It may be when you least expect it. But you'll know when the time is right. And that, my dear, is the moment to seize your fantasy."

2

ANTHONY MICHAEL MORETTI tucked the cell phone between his shoulder and his ear, trying to balance as he tugged on a pair of black jeans.

"So, come on, buddy," Alan insisted, his voice clear and strong despite being filtered through satellites and all sorts of digital technology. "Fess up. Was I right? Wasn't some R and R exactly what you needed?"

Tony chuckled, realizing how much he'd missed his best friend's needling over the past week. For eight months, he'd been living in hell, and Alan had been the one bright spot in his life. Certainly Amy hadn't been there for him. Despite sharing an apartment for two years, she'd run far and fast the day he'd come home from the hospital after the accident.

"The R and R's been great," Tony said. "Really." And it had. But the fact was, even though he'd come on this vacation for some rest and relaxation, he'd ended up getting a hell of a lot more than he'd bargained for.

Thanks to Merrilee, when darkness covered the island, he felt almost whole again. And about that, he couldn't complain. But during the daytime...well, in the light of day he was the same old Tony, a scarred and broken man.

"I told you an island getaway was just what you needed. Hell, Moretti. Beaches full of bikini-clad babes soaking up the sun..." He made a rough sound in the back of his throat. "No wonder they call the place a fantasy resort."

"True enough," Tony answered noncommittally, shifting the cell phone so he could rummage through the clothes strewn about the floor of his secluded cabana. It seemed like everything he owned was either black or white, which made it that much harder to find what he was looking for.

"Man, oh, man." Alan continued. "I sent you to that island when I coulda sent myself. You're not the only one who could use a little mindless vacationing."

"So come join me."

"Ha! And steal all the chicks away from you? No way."

Tony smiled, knowing full well that Alan was only ribbing him. More than anyone, Alan knew how badly the accident had shaken Tony. And when long talks, beer and bad movies hadn't done the trick, Alan had moved on to other forms of therapy. Never in a million years would his buddy have given himself such a potentially peaceful vacation. But the second Alan had decided that Tony needed some therapeutic down time...well, once he got an idea in his head, there was no talking him out of it.

At first, Tony had been hesitant. Even if he were healthy, hanging out on an island sounded duller than watching clothes dry. Considering he was scarred and on pain killers, the idea of basking in the sun seemed positively morbid. But Alan was convinced, and rather than disappoint his already worried friend, Tony had reluctantly agreed.

"You still there?" Concern laced Alan's voice, and guilt twitched in Tony's stomach. This trip was on Alan's dime, after all. He should make an effort to sound more upbeat.

"I'm here. I was…uh…watching the beach. Some girls playing volleyball."

Alan let loose a wolf whistle. "Aha! I was right, wasn't I? Hell, you already sound one hundred percent better." He paused. "You are doing better, right?"

"Yeah," Tony said, not sure if the answer was the truth or a lie. Maybe a little of both. "I'm doing okay."

"I'm glad to hear it, buddy." The line clicked. "Can you hold on a sec? That's probably my date about to cancel on me."

Tony laughed. "Sure. Wouldn't want you to miss that call."

With the silent phone pressed to his ear, Tony let his mind wander. What the hell was he doing? He'd come to Intimate Fantasy simply to calm a friend's concerns. So how had he ended up living out a secret fantasy that, seven days ago, he hadn't even known he had?

Yet somehow Merrilee had known what he needed.

Somehow she'd sorted through the mishmash of information on those zillions of forms, and managed to come up with his fantasy.

And for that, he'd always be grateful.

Maybe it wasn't real. Maybe it was all pretend, but somehow, in a small way, she'd given him his life back.

The accident had been bad, true, but he could live with the pain. What he couldn't live with was what had come after—the pitying looks when friends and strangers saw the freshly scarred flesh near his eye, then the damn suits saying he and his bad back couldn't return to work. *Permanent disability.* Bile rose in his throat as he remembered the official yellow envelope that had come in the mail only three months after the accident.

His whole life, he'd wanted to be a fire fighter, and he'd worked hard getting there. It was what he did, who he was. But after the accident, that was all ripped away. Instead of getting back into the saddle as he'd hoped, he'd spent the months after the hospital festering in his cramped apartment, splitting his time between watching bad daytime television and lashing out at Alan for lack of a better scapegoat.

He could work a desk, or take a white-collar consulting job, but, dammit, that wasn't the life he'd made for himself. No matter how he sliced it, filling out forms in triplicate wasn't going to save lives.

Through no fault of his own, his life had been ripped to shreds. He'd gone from being heroic, to being pathetic. From being needed, to being useless. He hated it.

The city's shrink had said the anger was normal. Maybe so, but Tony wasn't angry at the building for burning or the arsonist who set it. No, Tony'd been angry at the world. And somehow Merrilee had understood.

When he'd arrived at Fantasies, Inc., they'd had dinner and she'd passed him a neatly wrapped box. "A possibility," she'd said, in response to his questioning look. "If you want to simply relax in the shadows by the pool, that's your business. But there's a second chance in there. A chance to be someone else." She'd shrugged elegant shoulders. "Or maybe even to be yourself."

For two days the box had sat unopened in his cabana, but then—

"Yo! Tony! The babes still playing volleyball?"

Alan's irritated voice pulled him back. "Sorry. What?"

"I asked if you're looking forward to your last week?"

"Yeah," Tony said, absently, as his eyes scanned the floor for the object he'd been searching for. The sun was setting. Where the hell was it?

"Well, I gotta go. Miracle of miracles, we're still on for tonight. Dinner and a movie. Am I original, or what?"

"You're one of a kind."

"Yeah, well, I'll call you in a couple of days," Alan said. "Check on your tan. See if you've hooked up with some island beauty. That would do you a world of good."

"Right," he said absently as Alan hung up, even though what he wanted to say was *not damn likely*.

The Tony Moretti who'd practically been the poster boy for the Cranston Township's annual bachelor auction didn't exist anymore. That was simply the cold, hard truth.

Besides, Alan had it wrong. It wasn't just a woman Tony needed. It was something bigger, yet somehow intangible, some primal need that Merrilee had managed to awaken.

Of course, Alan didn't know the full story, and Tony wasn't inclined to confess all now. Easier to just let Alan believe that Tony was out and about, painting the town and getting it on with the ladies, healing his bruised ego with mythical women who didn't care about his face.

Alan was right. That would be any man's fantasy. Why muddy the waters by letting Alan know it wasn't his?

Thanks to Merrilee's package, Tony'd managed to become a familiar face on the island, so to speak. He was a hero again.

It may not have completely filled the hole in his gut, but he damn sure liked the feeling.

And he sure as hell didn't intend to mess it up by

getting involved with a woman who'd want to know the truth, then would run from it just like Amy had. Some things were meant to stay hidden. Some people were meant to stay alone.

Alan would just have to look elsewhere for sordid stories of female conquests.

"There you are," he whispered, finally finding what he'd been looking for—the single black eye patch that, along with a black cap and one vivid green contact lens, had made up the contents of Merrilee's present.

He stood in front of the mirror and nodded at his reflection, hating the hideous scar that edged his left eye. The flesh was no longer tender, but it still looked raw. To Tony, it was as raw as ever.

A red-hot steel bar had fallen with the collapsing roof. He'd thrown his body clear, wrenching his back out in the process. As if that injury wasn't enough, the rod had bounced up, cracking him in the face and gouging the tender flesh.

Despite legions of doctors, his prognosis wasn't exactly inspiring. His back was permanently screwed up, and his doctor had ruled out plastic surgery for his face, citing Tony's allergies and some other mumbo jumbo from Tony's medical history. *Sorry, kid, but just remember how lucky you are to be alive. Count your blessings, boy.*

Some luck.

Slowly, as if performing an ancient ritual, he lifted the eye patch to his face. The scars disappeared. He put in the single contact lens, then slicked gel through his hair, darkening it. When he put on the cap, he was a new person. A different person.

Tony Moretti was gone. Only a hero remained.

STUART PULLED the Jeep up in front of the restaurant and tapped the horn, which wasn't really necessary since Kyra was standing right there. "Ready to head on back?"

She fidgeted on the stone steps. "I don't know. I'm thinking about walking."

Frowning, he killed the engine, though the headlights stayed on, cutting a bright path through the dark. "You sure? It's a long walk, and it smells like rain."

Sure enough, when she sniffed, Kyra picked up on a freshness in the heavy air, along with a hint of restraint. As if the clouds were holding back, waiting for just the right moment. She and nature, it seemed, had something in common. They were both about to burst from pent-up energy, near to exploding in a torrent of need and desire.

"I'm sure," she said. "I don't mind a little rain." She welcomed it, in fact. She'd spent far too much of the evening daydreaming about Stuart's mysterious Michael, and as the hours wore on, her libido was ratcheting tighter and tighter. If she didn't cool off just a little, she'd probably launch herself at the next man she saw before he could even say "How do you do?"

Of course, ravaging unsuspecting male guests probably qualified as a bit more adventurous than Merrilee intended. Still, the thought wasn't typical of Kyra's usually calm and reasonable self, and she suppressed a smile. Maybe the fantasy was already working.

Stuart tapped his fingers on the steering wheel, catching her attention, then looked pointedly toward the sky.

"I'm walking," she said. "My mind's made up."

He didn't look happy, but he didn't argue. Instead, he mumbled "Whatever," and nodded in the general direction of her cabana. "Just don't get lost." He tossed her a windbreaker from the back seat.

She caught it with one hand. "Thanks."

"You won't be thanking me if it rains. That thing will barely keep you dry."

"I'll be fine."

"Hey, the customer is always right," he said, sliding the Jeep into gear, "even when the customer is soaking wet."

He pulled out, and Kyra followed in the same direction until she could no longer see the restaurant behind her. Her cabana was on the west beach, and as soon as she saw the little wooden arrow pointing down the footpath, she turned off the main road.

The gravel walkway that wound toward her beach was lined with small footlights. A slight breeze had kicked up, and now the wind rustled through her skirt, causing it to flutter behind her as the stones crunched underneath her sandals.

Like the rest of the island, the nearby flora had been only slightly tamed. Native flowers lined the walk, and the glow from the recessed lights cast a magical tinge over the entire area.

Kyra followed the curving path, breathing in the tropical perfume, then ran her finger over a Bird of Paradise. The flower was aptly named. Certainly, this island was a paradise, and she had one entire week to enjoy it.

She intended to savor every luscious moment.

She walked along, her body absorbing the heady tropical beat, tuning in to the island's sensual rhythms. In the distance, a flash of lightning ripped the sky, setting the trees and shrubs into eerie relief. Kyra jumped as a rumble of thunder followed. The air hung heavy, and she slipped the windbreaker on over her sundress.

After a while, the jungle-like foliage thinned, revealing the rear of her cabana and the peaceful spread of sand, now glowing under the fading light of the moon. The image was mystical, serene, and she remembered her first impression—a perfect place for a fantasy.

Once again, her mind turned to the adventure-filled fantasy Merrilee had mapped out for her—and the man she would share it with.

Who would he be? How would his hands feel? Strong and rough, or smooth and gentle? Would he touch her without invitation, taking what she gave without asking, but somehow knowing her innermost wishes? Or would he make her speak the words, urging her to reveal sensual secrets, things she'd never yet told a living soul.

Either way, he would be special. A man with whom she would have no secrets, but also no history. A man who would know everything about her, and yet know nothing. A man with whom she could lose herself, in whose arms she could forget her responsibilities, her worries, even her future.

As if in harmony with her thoughts, the air crackled, on the verge of releasing a thousand volts of untamed energy as wild as Kyra wanted to feel. Hoping to beat the storm, she hurried toward the back of her cabana. The world brightened as lightning again lit the sky— and something small, black and very fast scurried across the path right in front of her.

"Oh!" Kyra jumped, her hand to her chest. When her heart slowed, she realized it was just a cat, its green eyes glowing from below the broad leaves of a lush island plant.

"Well, hey there, baby."

It hissed and backed up, eyes narrowed to slits. The sky lit up just long enough for Kyra to see the gash on its ear.

"Poor thing. Were you in a fight? Do you want some food?" The cabana had a well-stocked kitchenette. Surely there was some tuna fish in one of the cabinets.

Large drops splattered on the path, still far enough

apart that Kyra could practically dodge them. Soon, though, the rain would be coming down with a vengeance.

Above her, mountainous clouds rumbled, bits of light dancing through the billows. Despite the impending deluge, she got down on her knees and patted the ground in front of her. The kitty started toward her, but then, in the wake of another flash, turned around and ran up a nearby tree.

"Well, great." She considered forgetting the whole thing and heading back to her cabana. Clearly the cat wasn't looking for company.

But as she started to walk away, it started howling, its pitiful mewls drifting down from the tree's top branches. Kyra tilted her head back and scowled. The cat looked totally stuck and determined not even to try to climb down. When the skies opened, the poor thing was going to get soaked unless Kyra managed to get it out of that tree.

With a frown, she aimed a longing glance toward her cozy cabana, then looked back up into the kitty's eyes. "You're going to owe me one, you know."

The old Kyra would probably have run into the cabana to avoid the storm, then called island security or something to take care of the poor cat. The new Kyra, however...

Saving a kitty wasn't going to earn her a spot on a Fox Network special about adventurous women, but maybe it was a start.

INTIMATE FANTASY was laid out like a wagon wheel, with the business offices, recreational areas, and restaurant at the center. The main and only paved road crossed the diameter, and the remaining spokes of the wheel were made up of dirt roads, some more rustic than others, leading to the various cabanas for the guests and permanent staff.

Already, Tony knew every path, every shadow, and he ran through a mental map of the island as he circled the old mission-turned-restaurant. By now, his beat was familiar. Once around each of the buildings, checking out the shadows, once to each of the pools and hot tubs, then finally down the main road to the beach. With a diameter of less than two miles across, the entire perimeter of the island was well under eight miles around. He could make the rounds in two hours, then stroll along the pathways until exhaustion carried him back to his own cabana.

Tonight was quiet—metaphorically, anyway. He'd hardly seen another human, much less anyone needing his help. The storm, probably. The couples were enjoying nature's pyrotechnics from the lush comfort of their private rooms. The single guests were most likely gathered in the restaurant, hoping their own personal fantasy somehow involved the storm of the century.

Tony was walking the west beach, sticking close to the tree line, his ears pricked for any sign of someone in trouble.

Truth be told, he was pretty sure the crises he'd

averted weren't completely random. After he'd saved one of the restaurant waitresses from drowning in the pool, Merrilee had told him that the island's summer staff of mostly college kids tended to be less than careful, that they needed looking out for. "Maybe the full moon makes them careless," she'd said.

Tony had only nodded. Maybe it was true, maybe it wasn't. It just seemed a little odd that so many people got in so much trouble on the island. He'd only been on the island for seven days, and he'd already become a magnet for folks in trouble.

So far, he'd prevented quite a few drownings, extinguished a spreading campfire that the staff had built too close to the tree line, and rescued a young woman lost in the island's wild foliage. He'd even rid the pool of a snake that had decided to call the warm water home—an experience he didn't care to repeat.

A couple of large raindrops splattered on his cap, and he rubbed the moisture off his face, surprised as always to feel the unfamiliar five o'clock shadow that he would normally have shaved. The stubble was just one more layer of the disguise he'd adopted.

He didn't consider himself anyone's fool, and despite Merrilee's comments, Tony knew that the island's run of bad luck probably had more to do with him than it did with the moon. After all, Merrilee and a few of her trusted staff members—Danielle to help with the details, Stuart to spread the story and provide an alibi if needed—had put the illusion together. They'd set him up to be a mysterious hero who moved in stealth through the night. And what good was a hero without something heroic to do?

The first night he'd opened the package, he'd simply ignored the disguise. *For the hours between twilight and dawn*, the note said.

In Tony's mind, those hours weren't any different than daylight—lonely and quiet. But by the second night, curiosity and pride had gotten the better of him. And as soon as the sun dipped beyond the horizon, he'd dressed and gone out.

That very night he'd saved a guest who'd foolishly gone for a midnight swim. Her lover had fallen asleep on the beach and hadn't heard her cries for help when she became entangled in some fishing line.

The woman's thank-you's had seemed genuine enough, but the next day he'd asked Merrilee. She'd merely shrugged. "The woman is alive. How much more real do you expect it to be?"

It was a non-answer and, to Tony, almost a confession that she was pulling the strings.

Still, he'd never know for sure. The woman had truly been trapped. It had taken all his strength to hold her above water and free her. And the little boy he'd saved a few days ago from a capsized boat had swallowed nearly half the ocean.

In the end, Tony didn't know where the setup ended and reality began. For him, at least, that meant everything was real. It was certainly real enough every morning when he popped a pain killer and iced down his aching back. And there was no faking the swell of pride and satisfaction he got from helping out, even if just a little.

As if on cue, a shrill scream cut through the night air, and Tony strained to pinpoint the source of the sound.

He couldn't hear anything now. Just the crash of waves kicked up by the oncoming storm, the low growl of thunder rippling across the sky, and the vibrant rustling of foliage tossed about by the wind.

Nature was about to put on a hell of a show. Whoever had screamed wasn't going to be too happy to be stuck in the middle of it.

From where he was, he couldn't see a damn thing. Frustrated, he ran toward the nearby cabana, then used an oddly tilted palm tree as a stepping stool. Ignoring the ever-present ache in his back, he hoisted himself up to the rooftop for a better view.

Lightning crackled overhead, and he saw her then— a woman hanging upside down by her knees from a single branch of a majestic tree near where the footpath opened up onto the beach. Her skirt hung loose over her face, and the quick view he had of her legs and stomach before the light faded was damned enticing.

A tiny black cat with wide green eyes perched a few feet away from her, calmly bathing itself at the base of the branch. Tony grinned at the irony. Despite the stereotype, during his firefighting days he'd never once rescued a kitten from a tree, much less a woman.

He climbed down then rushed over to her tree, accidentally stepping on a crumpled windbreaker she must have shed. "You okay?"

He heard a muffled reply as she reached up, unsuccessfully trying to hold her skirt over her legs and underwear. The material was thin, but it was wet and didn't want to cooperate. Most of it stayed plastered over her face.

Not that she needed to worry. The footlights didn't reach high enough to illuminate the little acrobat at all. Except for the one quick glance—courtesy of a cooperative bolt of lightning—her modesty was quite well protected.

"Miss?" As he always did on his night patrols, he pitched his voice lower than normal.

"I'm upside down," she said, sounding far away from behind the wet fabric.

He put his hand over his mouth to hide his smile. "So I see."

"Great. My heroic knight does stand-up."

He still couldn't see her face, but from the mix of amusement and irritation lacing her voice, he imagined she was rolling her eyes.

"Do you want me to help you down?"

"Whatever for? I'm perfectly comfortable."

Her soft Southern accent seemed out of place against her biting sarcasm, and he laughed, now even more intrigued.

"Uh-huh. Okay. I guess I'll head on back before the

skies open up." He turned and started walking down the footpath, kicking up gravel so she was sure to hear him go.

"Wait!"

"Yes?"

"Maybe you could give me a hand, since you're here and all."

"You're sure? I'd hate to destroy any illusions you have about modern-day chivalry."

Silence. Then, "Sorry. I get snippy when I'm embarrassed. It's nothing personal."

"Lady, I never take women hanging upside down and flashing their underwear at me personally."

This time, her laugh was genuine, and she shook so much that her legs slipped a bit on the tree.

He braced to catch her, but she managed to steady herself.

"Um, maybe you could give me that hand now."

He grinned, moving to stand under her. "As you wish." She fumbled with the material stuck to her face, pushing it aside to reveal exotic eyes. They reflected the lights from the path, and despite a tinge of fear, her slate-gray irises sparkled with a zest and openness he found completely refreshing.

For a second, she just stared at him, her brow furrowed, then her eyes went wide. "It's you."

"Me?" His stomach roiled. Did she know him?

"Stuart's mysterious Mr. Michael."

He exhaled in relief. This woman didn't know Tony

Moretti, just his alter ego's reputation, thanks to Stuart's efforts to sing Michael's praises. His secret was still safe.

"Why don't we do the socializing once your feet are on the ground?"

She nodded—more or less, anyway. "What do you want me to do?"

That was a good question. Normally he'd climb up the tree, but with the drizzle, the wood would be slick, and he wasn't at all sure he could make it up there, much less get her down. "Can you get turned around? Reach up and catch the branch?"

"I tried. I can't seem to do it. In high school, my only failing grade was in gym."

"Then we've only got one choice. Do you trust me?"

She caught his eye, her lips pressed tight together. "Yes," she said, after the briefest hesitation.

He felt a surprising surge of pleasure sweep through him. Foolish. He didn't know the woman, had no reason to care about what she thought of him. But still, there it was.

His career had trained him to compartmentalize his emotions. To just get the job done. The accident honed that skill. He could analyze his reaction to the woman later. Right now he needed to focus on the problem at hand.

"I want you just to let go."

"Excuse me?" Her voice rose to near hysterical proportions. "Are you nuts?"

"If you can't pull yourself up, it's the only way down." He kept his voice level, reasonable. "I can't climb up there in the rain, and there's no time to run get a ladder. Your knees have got to be getting tired, and the tree's only going to get more slick."

She mumbled something he couldn't make out.

"I'll catch you," he promised, hoping his temperamental back wouldn't make a liar out of him. "You said you trusted me."

"I do. But I'm not exactly Calista Flockhart. I've had a long-standing love affair with glazed donuts, and I'm not sure you can catch all of me."

Considering he'd carried guys weighing over two hundred pounds out of burning buildings, he wasn't too worried. His back was an issue, of course, but since he fully intended to ignore the pain, he decided not to mention that. Besides, he'd caught a nice view of her earlier, and from where he was standing she looked to be just about the perfect size for a woman.

"I think I'm blushing," she said when he told her so.

"I think you're stalling," he countered.

"Well, yeah, maybe. Like I said, it's nothing personal."

He had to grin. The woman was upside down, but still worrying about hurting his feelings. He tried to come up with some other options, but no brilliant alternative solution leaped to mind. "You're going to get tired and fall anyway," he said. "You might as well let me catch you."

He saw fear, then resignation. "You won't drop me?"

He reached up, his fingertips brushing hers. "Never."

A muscle moved in her throat. She nodded. "Okay."

"On three," he said. "One. Two."

"Three." They said the word in unison, and he braced as she let herself fall backward.

Before he could react, she was in his outstretched arms. White-hot fingers of pain shot up his back, and he stumbled on the uneven ground. But he didn't break his promise. He didn't drop her.

"Thank you." Still in his arms, she smiled up at him, her gray eyes wide and her breath coming in small, quick gasps. He held her close to his body, the pulse of his heart echoing against her. Impulsively, he pressed a quick kiss to her forehead, breathing in the subtle scent of strawberries. Most of her hair had escaped its ponytail holder, and now it tangled wild and wet around her face.

His first thought was that she was beautiful. His second, that she was dangerous. Hell, even with his back, he felt like he could stand there forever, just holding her.

Oh, yeah. She was dangerous.

She shifted, the movement against him igniting a powerful physical reaction.

Very, very dangerous.

"You can put me down." Her voice was soft, as if she

somehow realized that speaking would destroy the moment. He mentally cringed. There was no *moment*, no anything. He'd simply helped an attractive woman out of a bind.

"Right," he answered, his back celebrating the decision.

Once her feet were firmly on the ground, she smiled, almost formally, as if she, too, was trying to shake off a queer sense of connection. "Well. I, uh, should introduce myself." She stuck her hand out. "I'm Kyra. Kyra Cartwright."

He hesitated, knowing that if he took her hand he'd feel it again. That surge of power, that shock to the senses. Maybe women weren't on his current agenda, but if he shook her hand, he knew—somehow, he just *knew*—that, woman or no, Kyra Cartwright would end up penciled in.

What the hell. He closed his fingers around hers, satisfying some deep, primal need to simply touch her.

She licked her lips, her eyes drifting to their interlocked hands. With a gentle tug, she pulled her hand free, the brush of her skin against his like the softest silk. Instead of meeting his eyes, she looked up into the tree. "Guess I risked my neck for nothing."

He followed her gaze and realized that the cat had disappeared.

"I'm sure the kitten appreciated your efforts."

"Maybe. But I hope it doesn't expect a bowl of cream

if it shows up at my door after getting me stuck like that."

He took a step toward her, noting with pleasure that she didn't move back. "I bet you'd give it some anyway."

"Yeah. I probably would." She met his gaze head on, this time smiling. "I guess I'm just a sucker."

"Not at all."

He saw a thousand questions dance across her face, but she asked none of them. Instead, she simply stood on her tiptoes, kissed his cheek and whispered, "Thank you."

Even after she'd stepped away, the feathery touch of her lips lingered on his skin, as if he'd been softly branded. She was smiling, almost shyly, and his stomach twisted as he wondered if she'd be so quick to kiss him if she knew the truth about him. If she'd seen the real Tony under the mask.

He stifled a sigh. The bottom line was that he'd helped her, and she'd looked at him like a hero, not like a pariah.

She saw him as the man he used to be, not the broken man he'd become. Everything he wanted, everything he needed, was right there in her eyes.

But not one bit of it was real.

No wonder he still felt so hollow.

3

MORTIFIED.

Kyra was one hundred percent, fully loaded, no-holds-barred, mortified.

Over the course of twenty-six years, she'd had plenty of opportunities to do embarrassing things. But hanging upside down with her underwear fluttering in the breeze pretty much took first prize. Especially when she was baring it all in front of a gorgeous man whose whiskey-smooth voice made her blood race and her toes curl. A man who could well be the walking, talking embodiment of her fantasy.

She'd kissed his cheek without thinking—isn't that what girls who needed rescuing did?—and that had been a big mistake. He smelled like the ocean breeze that had been teasing her all day. And the sandpaper-ish touch of his cheek against her mouth left her lips tingling, left her wanting more—and the realization unnerved her.

He was dark and mysterious and intriguing, and she felt like a high-school girl thrust into close quarters with the varsity quarterback.

Stop it! She'd come here wanting a fantasy, and here

it was—here *he* was. She needed to pull herself together. Needed to remember how to act sexy and sophisticated—just the way all those articles in *Cosmo* laid it out. That's what she needed to do.

So why the heck was she so terrified? Why hadn't she realized this would be so hard?

And what if she made an advance and he wasn't the least bit interested in her? *That* would certainly ratchet her mortification level up to monumental proportions. And why would he be interested? After all, since she was acting like a teenager, that's probably just how he thought of her—a flighty airhead who needed a man around to keep her out of trouble. Of course, considering he'd just rescued her from a tree, maybe that wasn't too absurd an assumption.

Absently, she smoothed her skirt. "I...I don't usually do such stupid things." She wanted him to realize she wasn't a space cadet.

"Trying to help a cat out of a bind?"

She glanced up and saw his grin despite the darkness and shadows hiding his face. "No. Getting stuck like that. I'm usually more self-reliant. Really."

"Nothing wrong with needing a little help every once in a while."

"No, there's not." Heck, she was planning to marry Harold because she needed a little help. So she certainly wasn't going to argue with his philosophy. "I just wasn't really expecting—"

She clamped her mouth shut, remembering Merrilee's words. *It may be when you least expect it...* Her knees went weak as she tried to get her mind around what was going on. He was her rescuer, her hero, her fantasy...and that scared her to death.

He moved closer, and his arm closed around her, warm and possessive. "Are you okay?"

She nodded, realizing only then that she was shivering.

"Hmmm." He didn't sound convinced. "After hanging upside down like that, I shouldn't have let you stand up."

The deep timbre of his voice shot straight through her, pooling somewhere between her thighs. Oh, Lord, she needed to get a grip. No matter how enticing he might be, no matter how much she wanted this fantasy, it was all happening too fast. Just five minutes ago, she'd been upside down, for crying out loud.

She needed to let her head clear. Her fingers practically itched for her notebook and pen. She wanted to step back, to analyze, to weigh the pros and the cons. To figure out what she should do next.

She never moved this quickly, and for the first time she feared that she'd made a huge mistake coming to Fantasies, Inc. She'd lived her whole life a certain way. Calm and ordered, she'd been the rock. The one everyone could trust, the one they relied on not to jump in without thinking. What demon had possessed her body when she'd filled out that application?

The same demon who was now whispering in her

ear, urging her to jump into his arms, to press her lips against his, to—

She shook her head, hoping to order her thoughts.

"I'm fine. Really." She moved against his arm, trying to get free, but he held fast, his hold both unnerving and enticing.

"Let me walk you to your cabana."

She surprised herself by not resisting, and he steered them forward along the path, moving as if they'd walked that way together a thousand times.

He seemed so *right*. The way they fit together, the way they moved, and with each step, a layer of fears and hesitations slipped away.

She'd left the lights on, and in the distance her cabana looked warm and inviting against the dark, damp night. Kyra sped up, drawn to the light, hoping against hope that moving away from the magical illumination of the lightning storm and into the harsh reality of incandescent bulbs would somehow bring her back to her senses.

Was she really thinking about inviting him inside?

Oh, yeah. She really was. And the realization was terrifying.

"Wait," he said behind her.

She stopped, turning around to face him. "What is it?" She tried to read his face, but the night hid his expression.

"Not into the light." He moved back, under the cover of a palm tree.

Curious, she followed him into the shadows, sharing the concealing darkness with him like lovers might share a blanket.

"You take my breath away," he whispered. His voice was low, barely audible under the rush of wind through the palm fronds. "I don't know if this is such a good idea."

"If what's a good idea?" she asked. It was a stupid question. She knew with absolute certainty exactly what he meant.

"This." He reached out, then stroked her cheek with the edge of his thumb. She trembled as he traced the contour of her face. Slowly, sensually, the movement of flesh against flesh ignited her blood, sending it to pool in her belly, her thighs.

"Oh." Her voice shook. "That. Right. Of course." She seemed to have lost control of her thoughts and voice. Never in her life had she experienced such a swell of longing for another person. Never before had she wanted to throw herself into a man's arms and abandon rational thought to the sweet sensations generated by the press of his body against hers.

The swell of desire terrified as much as it excited Kyra. Her logical mind knew it was just chemistry. His pheromones calling to her pheromones. But that didn't change the fact that she seemed to be teetering on the edge of a precipice, and if she lost her balance, she'd surely fall.

"Probably not a good idea at all," she agreed, but didn't move away.

"Probably not." The deep rumble of his voice touched her in secret places, warming her soul. He didn't stop touching her, and she closed her eyes, savoring the moment, afraid it would end and yet more afraid it would continue.

Almost unconsciously, she moved closer, seeking more of his heat. His finger traced the curve of her neck, then skimmed the edge of her collarbone. His free arm circled her waist, pulling her closer. She shivered, not from cold or fear, but from the flurry of uncontrollable sensations racing through her.

Her pulse beat against her throat, and she focused on slowing her racing heart, suddenly unsure and more than a little uncomfortable.

She didn't know the woman standing under a tree with this mysterious stranger. Certainly that woman wasn't the Kyra Cartwright she knew. Kyra Cartwright never did anything so...so...*spontaneous.*

But maybe this was the woman who needed a fantasy. Who needed an escape. Who needed to see what else life had to offer. Maybe this was the woman who'd gathered her courage and bought a vacation from Fantasies, Inc.

He leaned forward, his proximity dizzying. "Kyra?" His voice caressed her, his breath hot against her ear. "Tell me what you want."

Lord help her, she wanted him. And the feeling

whipped through her like a hurricane—wild, untamed and terribly frightening.

She'd purchased a fantasy vacation that she'd assumed she could walk away from. A week of hedonism—or near hedonism, anyway—and then she'd be back to normal. This longing in her gut would be out of her system. And she'd go back to Harold and the rest of her life.

Was she an idiot? Had she been a fool to think she could just walk away?

She gnawed on her lip, her insides twisting, not at all sure that hedonism was her thing after all.

The wind lashed out as she broke free from his embrace, determined to batten down the hatches and ride out the storm raging inside her.

Gathering her courage, she drew in a fortifying breath, then reached up to capture his hand in hers. "I should go."

He nodded, his sadness almost palpable, but his relief unmistakable. "Yes." His lips curved in an ironic smile. "You should."

She nodded, then started to back away. But before she could put any distance between them, he stepped forward. In one bold, possessive movement, he gripped the sides of her arms, gently, yet firmly. Her breath quickened as he closed the distance between them, every atom in her being telling her to put a stop to this right now, that he would lead her someplace dangerous. Dangerous for her heart, confusing for her head.

She needed to walk away but, heaven help her, she couldn't.

She wanted it, and when his mouth closed over hers, she could only moan as her body melted into his.

HE WAS A JERK.

So much for respect, so much for chivalry, so much for all those social niceties his mother had tried so hard to drill into his head. Every single one of them had flown straight out the window. He'd kissed her, and damn it all, he didn't regret it for a minute.

Her mouth moved under his, soft and sweet and delicious. She moaned, a sexy little noise in the back of her throat, and the sound just about undid him.

His body hummed under the press of her curves against him. They fit together perfectly, her hips tucked against his, her breasts, round and firm against his chest.

He wanted her. Despite everything he'd told himself in his cabana only hours earlier, he wanted her. This woman. This moment.

A primitive urge raced through him with so much force it left him breathless. His erection strained against his jeans and he knew that she could feel him, could tell exactly how much he craved her.

He moved, just slightly, brushing against her and forcing himself not to groan from the sheer, decadent agony. Her mouth tasted richer than wine, and he urged her lips apart, wanting to taste her, wanting to know everything about her.

She opened her mouth to his, taking what he offered, sharing herself with him. She was passionate and sweet and perfect—and she was there in his arms. He felt dizzy from the wonder of it. She was with him. She wanted him just as much as he wanted her.

She shifted against him, her little noises driving him nuts, and then her hands were in his back pockets, urging him closer. He wanted to lose himself, to be as close to her as possible, and then even closer still. He wanted to wrap her around him like a blanket. To forget everything except the exquisite pleasure of this woman in his arms.

Except it was all a lie. Every bit of it.

The truth weighed down on him, and he broke the kiss. Pulling her close, he buried his face in her hair, seeking the strength to move away. This was wrong. He was weak, foolish.

For months he'd been living alone, telling himself it didn't matter that Amy left, that women didn't even look in his direction anymore. But it did matter. God help him, it did.

A wave of sadness crashed over him. It was all an illusion. She wasn't there with Tony Moretti. Hell, she didn't even know Tony Moretti. If she knew the truth, she'd run far and fast.

With a massive effort, he summoned his strength. "Kyra, I—"

"Please. No." She backed away, gently freeing herself from the bonds of his arms. Her gaze flicked up to his face, then down to the path. "We shouldn't... This isn't... I want to, but..." She looked up, her eyes brimming with tears. "I'm sorry," she said. Then she turned and ran into her cabana without looking back.

He watched her go, waiting on the path until the door closed behind her. Then he waited even longer for the lights to fade and for darkness to envelop her cabana. The drizzle grew into rain, the wind lashing around him as the inevitable storm approached.

Still he stood there watching, the sadness in his gut almost nauseating.

Disgusted, he ripped off his cap and the cursed eye patch. Damn Merrilee. She'd given him everything he'd ever wanted. But she'd only given him a taste. Just enough to whet his appetite. Just enough for him to remember how much he'd lost.

KYRA WOKE UP to sunshine, a melted candy bar stuck to her face and tangled in her hair, and a pounding headache.

She felt disoriented and vaguely sad. It took her a moment to remember why, and then it hit her—*him*. Michael.

After she'd raced away—conjuring every ounce of self-control to keep from turning back and begging him to follow—she'd satisfied her raging hormones with wine, chocolate and a few pages from a favorite romance novel. Apparently, she hadn't quite finished the candy.

Sitting up, she wiped chocolate off her cheek and tucked the tangled, gooey hair mess behind her ear. Sadness didn't even begin to cover it. She felt empty. All because she'd walked away from him. But it had been the right choice.

Hadn't it?

Nibbling on her lower lip, she padded into the bathroom and stared herself down in the mirror. She looked a sight. Hair hanging in chocolate clumps, pillow creases on her face, and a candy smear all up her cheek.

Michael certainly wouldn't want her now. She didn't look a thing like the romantic damsel in distress. And that's all it had been—just a moment of passion brought on by an intense situation, nothing real at all. She should forget about it—about him—and get on with the business of her fantasy.

She turned the tap on the bathtub, letting it run as she took a washcloth and scrubbed at her face.

Her reflection stared back at her, and she scowled. "It's good you ran away."

Her reflection didn't look convinced.

"Really." She closed her eyes, trying to convince herself she'd done the right thing. No matter how much she'd anticipated this trip, no matter how much she'd craved him, no matter how much her skin had burned under his touch, no matter how much she'd longed to feel his hands on her bare skin...

She shivered under the onslaught of memories, cursing herself for running away, even while congratulating herself for doing the right thing. Opening her eyes, she frowned at her reflection. No question about it, she'd done the right thing. Right? *Right.*

Maybe.

Sighing, she planted her hands on either side of the sink and leaned in toward the mirror. She needed to talk this one out. She'd have to go see Merrilee.

After a bath to loosen the chocolate and a shower to get rid of it, she dried her hair, then pulled it back into a sloppy ponytail. She climbed back into her sundress—dry, but still a bit wrinkled from her adventure—then grabbed a sweatshirt from behind the bathroom door and pulled it on.

Not exactly haute couture, but why did she need to dress up just to run to the administration office?

Besides, dressing like a slob was a bit of its own adventure. In Dallas, she wouldn't be seen dead without her perfectly tailored clothes. So this little bit of fashion rebellion was empowering. *So would a fling with Michael.* She scowled, trying to ignore that opinionated little voice.

Determined, she shoved her feet into a pair of Keds, threw her cabana key and notebook into a tote bag, and headed out into the humid island air. By the time she'd trekked to the office, her hair had slipped free from her ponytail and little strands had plastered themselves to her face. She remembered her plan to buy barrettes, and made a quick note to stop by the gift store on her way back.

Merrilee's office was tucked away in a small building behind the restaurant, facing east—very modest, but with a view of the ocean that would make real estate developers drool. As Kyra rounded the corner, she saw the silhouette of a man against the morning sun. He was walking away, a lone figure on the beach. Something about him was familiar, but she couldn't place it. He definitely wasn't Michael.

Shrugging, she pushed open the glass-paneled French doors, then stepped hesitantly over the threshold into the airy reception area. Empty. Just her, a yellow cat snoozing on a file cabinet, and a single reception desk topped with the largest bouquet of ruby-red roses Kyra had ever seen.

"Hello?" Her voice echoed through the office. "Anyone here?"

Nothing. And then she heard the unmistakable sound of heels clicking on the boardwalk leading up to the office. Within seconds, Kyra saw Danielle, Merrilee's assistant, hurrying toward the door, her clipboard held out in front of her.

"Kyra!" she said when she looked up from the clipboard. "It's so good to see you." She noticed the flowers and frowned. Then she checked the card and a slow grin spread across her face.

She must have remembered what she was doing, because she turned back to Kyra, suddenly all business.

"Sorry. There's not a problem is there? With your room? With your fantasy?"

"No. Yes. I mean, not exactly." She nibbled on her lip, trying to remember what she'd so desperately wanted to ask Merrilee.

Danielle slid the clipboard onto the desk, then turned, giving Kyra her full attention. "Do you want to talk about it? Sometimes it takes guests a day or so to get used to a Fantasies, Inc. vacation. The staff is always ready to talk."

"I was kind of hoping to talk to Merrilee," Kyra confessed, hoping that Danielle's feelings wouldn't be hurt.

"I completely understand, but she's not here." She gestured to her spiffy business suit, complete with pumps and panty hose. "Trust me. I don't dress like this normally, not on an island. But we have a meeting with a possible new supplier. Merrilee took a boat over last night, and I'm meeting her there this morning."

"Oh. Well, it can wait." Besides, she wasn't even certain what she wanted to ask. Confirmation that Michael was her fantasy man? Permission to have a wild fling?

For that matter, did Merrilee already know that Kyra had blown her chance? That she hadn't seized the unexpected?

"Kyra?"

She shrugged and continued, "I guess I'm wondering how much Merrilee knows about what happens on the island."

Danielle actually giggled, a totally unexpected response. Apparently, she realized it, because she slapped her hand over her mouth, her eyes wide.

Kyra squinted, confused. "What's so funny?"

"Sorry." Danielle's gaze drifted to the flowers. "It's just that a few weeks ago I would have sworn that nothing could happen on any of the islands without Merrilee knowing. But now..." She trailed off, raising one shoulder in a tiny shrug.

Kyra looked from Danielle to the flowers, then back to Danielle. "A secret admirer?"

Danielle leaned forward and nodded conspiratorially. "She doesn't have a clue who he is. But I think it's great. Every couple of days he sends a little gift or roses. Ruby-red, the card always says, because those are her favorite."

"How mysterious!"

Danielle nodded, clearly trying to stay businesslike, but her grin gave her away. "I think it's great. Merrilee deserves to have someone making such a fuss over her. But it's driving her crazy trying to figure out who could be sending them." She cocked her head. "You didn't see who brought them, did you?"

"The flowers?"

"The desk was empty earlier. He must have come when I left to change into my business-girl getup."

"No, I—" Kyra stopped. "Wait. There was a man on the beach."

Danielle's cheeks flushed and she moved closer.

"Really? What did he look like? Was he tall? Handsome? Did you recognize him?"

Laughing, Kyra backed away, her hands held up. "Whoa! I didn't see anything. Sorry. He was too far away."

"Well, darn." She glanced wistfully toward the flowers. "I'm dying to know who her admirer is."

"Merrilee doesn't have any ideas?"

"Not a clue." Danielle hugged herself. "It's so romantic."

That it was, and a tiny kernel of jealousy sat like a stone in her stomach. Harold respected and desired her, but there wasn't any romance—no romantic gestures, no soft words that made her melt.

Of course, the truth was she didn't want those things. A romance needed two participants, and while she respected Harold—and even loved him in a friendly sort of way—she couldn't fathom getting all mushy about him.

But with Michael...well, *that* she could imagine just fine.

The thought came unbidden, and she cringed. The man had managed to work his way under her skin. She hadn't expected that, not while she'd been sitting in her brightly lit office in Dallas arranging the vacation. She shivered. She hadn't expected it at all.

"Will you let me know if you figure out who the man was?" Danielle asked.

She nodded absently. "Sure. Yeah. No problem."

"Did you want to talk to me? Or leave a note for Merrilee?"

"A note?" She frowned. "No. No thanks. I'm...I'll figure it out."

Danielle smiled, then went to a cabinet on the far side of the room, opened the wood paneled doors, and pulled out a cell phone. She passed it to Kyra. "Here."

"What's this for?"

"Intimate Fantasy doesn't have phones in the guest rooms. So we check these out to guests from time to time." She shrugged. "You don't have to use it. It's just that a lot of folks feel better after talking their fantasy through with a friend. It's not unusual at all. We have more people phoning a friend than the contestants on *Who Wants To Be A Millionaire?*"

Kyra nibbled on her lip, staring at the phone in the palm of her hand. The only one she could call was Mona, and Kyra knew exactly what her friend would say: *You turned down a wild night with a quintessential fantasy man? Are you nuts?*

No, Mona wouldn't be any help at all. But instead of giving the phone back, she surprised herself by tucking it into her tote bag. "Thanks."

"No problem. And Kyra," Danielle added, "remember what Merrilee says. Fantasies aren't a science. In the end, your fantasy is what you make it."

4

TONY SPRAWLED on one of the lounge chairs under an oversize beach umbrella that had been rigged to provide some shade near the pool. He'd hardly slept at all last night—his damsel in distress had haunted his dreams—and now he let the gentle sound of folks splashing in the pool and ordering drinks from the bar work on him like a lullaby.

Still, though, he couldn't sleep. Thoughts of Kyra teased and taunted him.

That morning, he'd awakened fully aroused, her scent on his clothes. A cold shower had relieved some of the pressure, but it hadn't changed one basic fact—he wanted her.

In a way, the feeling was welcome. He hadn't wanted a woman—hadn't let himself want a woman—since the accident. Certainly he had never let one get so close to him.

But it was a false closeness. She didn't really know him. She'd been attracted to the chivalrous green-eyed stranger with midnight black hair.

Only none of it was real.

Tony's own hair was near-black, but the gel made it

darker. His own face was scarred, and he'd hidden it under a patch, a cap, and an evening beard that he'd happily shaved off this morning. His own eyes were a bland shade of brown, one of which changed with the help of a vivid green contact lens. He even pitched his voice differently at night.

True, he'd helped her out of a bind. But his back could only take so much more of that, and he was paying the price this morning. Besides, they were in the middle of an island fantasy. Out in the real world, he was no heroic knight—not anymore. And all the good he did on this island was nothing but cotton candy—sweet enough, but ready to dissolve in an instant. The bottom line? Michael was nothing more than an illusion.

"Hey, Tony!"

He kept his eyes closed, feigning sleep.

"Yo! Moretti!" This time the shout was accompanied by the sound of splashing water, followed by a splattering of droplets all over him.

He sat up, then looked over the rim of his sunglasses into Stuart's smiling face.

"We're getting up a group to play some water volleyball. Want to join in?"

"No thanks."

Stuart hauled himself up and out of the pool, the sun gleaming on his golden hair. Unlike Tony, Stuart wasn't ever going to have a problem with women looking the other way.

He marched over, leaving a trail of wet footprints on the slate poolside. "You're just gonna sit here in the shade?"

Tony nodded, shifting so Stuart saw only the good side of his face. "Yup." Stuart had already seen the scars, and to his credit, he hadn't flinched. Tony didn't want to give him the chance to cringe now. "I'm just going to sit here in the shade."

Stuart plopped down in a chair opposite Tony. "Come on, guy? What fun is that? We're supposed to get another storm tonight that might even last into tomorrow. You should get out and get some sun while you can."

"I appreciate your concern for my tan, but I'm perfectly happy in the shade."

"Well, it's not just your tan, guy. We need one more person on our team."

Tony shook his head. No way was he dragging out the scar for all to see. No way was he going to reach up to slam-dunk a volleyball only to have his back blow out in front of everybody. Just wasn't happening. Not in this lifetime.

"You sure? We could really use—"

"Stuart," a deep voice interrupted, "the boy said no."

Tony tilted his head back to see C.J., the resort's pilot, striding over.

"Hey, C.J.," Stuart said, a little morosely. "But we need another player. How about you?"

"I don't think so." C.J. said, then laughed. He ducked under the umbrella and took the chair on Tony's bad side. Tony shifted, but there wasn't anywhere to go. In the end, he settled for pushing his sunglasses more firmly up his nose.

Now settled, C.J. peeled off his aviator glasses, revealing vivid blue eyes. Slight crow's-feet made C.J. seem constantly happy, even though the lines probably meant nothing more than that the man had spent too much time in the sun.

"Well, heck," Stuart said. He knew when he was defeated, though. His eyes immediately started searching the area around the pool for another victim.

Tony had just turned to C.J., when Stuart's hand flew up. "Kyra! Hey! Over here."

Tony's stomach twisted. *Kyra?* His Kyra? Calling on every ounce of strength in his body, he managed to maintain a bland expression as he turned to look at her climbing the steps to the pool area.

She was a vision, her honey-colored hair loose in the breeze. He watched as she impatiently pushed a long strand away from her face as she looked around to see who was calling her.

This time, she wasn't in a dress, but was wearing a pair of flower-print shorts with a jacket over what looked to be a matching swimsuit. The shorts hugged her hips, the top accentuated the swell of her breasts, and Tony tried to keep his breathing steady as he remembered the heavenly feel of every delicious inch of her pressed against him.

"Over here," Stuart called.

She waved, then headed in their direction—in his direction. Every muscle in his body stiffened, and he fought the urge to run, afraid somehow she'd recognize him, and then any chance that Michael Moretti might have of spending another night with her would be ruined.

Disgusted with himself, he stifled a groan. The truth was, she probably wouldn't even look twice at him. Surely she wouldn't recognize him.

With a determined tug, he pulled off his sunglasses and tossed them on the table. Then he pulled up the back of the lounge chair, and sat up to face her, determined to hold his own.

She headed right over, flashing a smile at his companions. "Hi, C.J. Hi, Stuart."

He was just about to mentally congratulate himself on reading her just right—she *was* going to ignore him—when her sleek gray eyes met his. She held out her hand, her head cocked slightly.

"Hi. I'm Kyra."

"Tony," he said, more gruffly than he intended. He took her outstretched hand. Any fantasy he'd held out that the sparks between them last night had been due to the lightning storm faded. Suddenly, there was just the two of them, her flesh against his, and he wanted to pull her close to him and wrap his arms around her almost as much as he wanted to yell at her to go away and never look at him again.

"Tony?" Stuart kicked the end of the lounge chair, and Tony realized he was still holding her hand. He dropped it.

She rubbed her hands together, her eyes still on his face. He could practically feel his scar burning under her critical stare.

"It's just a scar, okay?"

She blinked. "What?"

He pointed at it. "It's just a scar."

Her face cleared and a horrified expression crossed her face. "Oh! No. I'm sorry. I wasn't staring at...I mean..." She sucked in a deep breath. "It's just that you seem so familiar. Have we met?"

"No," he said quickly, shrinking to about two inches tall. "I'm sure I'd remember you."

Idiot, idiot, idiot. Not only had he completely misread her, but now what if she put two and two together?

Her forehead furrowed. "Maybe in the restaurant. I don't know. There's something..."

"Couldn't have been the restaurant," Stuart said, and Tony could practically see the wheels turning in his head. "Tony spent all of yesterday on one of the other islands. He only came back this morning."

"Scoping it out for a friend," Tony added, pleased that Merrilee's promise that Stuart and Danielle would back his alibi had held fast. "Perhaps we've seen each other earlier in the week?'' he suggested, knowing that was impossible, since she'd only just arrived.

She shook her head. ''No. I got here yesterday.'' Her smile was bright and sunny. ''Well, at any rate, it's nice to meet you now.''

''Very nice,'' Tony said, relaxing against the chair. His alibi was solid. Even if she wondered about his scar and Michael's patch, there's no way she'd catch on now. Merrilee did her job well.

''The game, you guys,'' Stuart said, almost pleading. ''It's waiting.''

Kyra frowned. ''What game?''

Stuart sighed, then jerked his head impatiently toward the pool, his mop of hair flying like a member of a sixties band. ''Volleyball. You're on my team.''

''Volleyball,'' she repeated, sounding almost horrified. ''Oh, no. I don't know how.'' She dug a cell phone out of her mesh tote bag. ''Besides, I was going to make a phone call.''

''Can't it wait?'' Stuart asked. ''Where are you calling?''

''Excuse me?'' She glanced at C.J. then Tony for help. He just shrugged, not at all opposed to watching Kyra in the pool.

''Where are you calling?''

''Texas,'' she said, then put her hand on her hip. ''Would you like a name and phone number?''

''Nah,'' Stuart said, either not hearing her irritation or ignoring it. ''It's just that they're an hour behind. So it's only ten there, and it's Sunday, so you oughta at least wait an hour. Let whoever you're calling sleep in and play a game or two with us."

Kyra looked mildly terrified. "But I've never...I don't know how."

Apparently Stuart took that as a yes, because he was up out of his chair and helping her off with her jacket. He tossed it Tony's way. "It's easy. You'll have a ball."

"Um, but..." She looked from Stuart to C.J., and then to Tony, her gaze lingering on him.

Tony grinned. "Have fun."

"Thanks. *You're* a lot of help."

That just made his smile broader, and as Stuart led her away, he realized how much he enjoyed being near her. He'd loved the feel of her in his arms last night, but he wanted more than just to have Kyra in his bed. A lot more. And he hadn't the faintest idea how to go about getting her.

"Nice girl," C.J. said, pulling Tony away from the enticing view of Kyra stripping off her shorts to reveal a matching swimsuit bottom.

"Hmm?"

C.J. chuckled. "I said, nice girl."

"Kyra?" Tony said, feigning nonchalance. "Yeah. I guess so."

"Give it up, son. You're talking to a man who's been infatuated with a woman once or twice in his life."

"I didn't realize I was so transparent." He glanced

toward the pool, wondering if Kyra'd been glad to get away from the scarred guy who had the hots for her.

"Don't worry, kid. I don't think she noticed."

"You read minds professionally? Or is it just a hobby?"

"I just recognize a kindred spirit when I see one." He gestured toward the bar. "I'm not flying today. Can I buy you a beer?"

"Sure."

The older man left for the bar as Tony wondered what he meant about kindred spirits. When C.J. came back with two ice-cold long necks, Tony didn't waste time letting the man sit down. "You've got a girl on one of the islands," he guessed.

The older man's eyes sparkled. "Got? No. But I'm working on it."

Tony leaned forward, his mind sifting through the possibilities. "Staff or guest?"

"What is this? Twenty questions?"

"Just curious." Tony genuinely liked this man. C.J. was one of those salt-of-the-earth guys, the kind who looked like they carried around a ton of baggage, yet never let it get to them. The kind of man who deserved to be genuinely off-the-scale happy, but always seemed to come in a few points short. "So who is she?"

"Not yet, buddy." C.J. took a long swallow of beer. "I like you, kid, I really do. And maybe one of these days I'll tell you. In the meantime, I'll keep your secret from Kyra if you keep mine to yourself, okay?"

Tony chuckled, but nodded, and they watched the game in companionable silence until C.J. stood up. "Time for me to go clean out the plane." He polished off the rest of his beer. "Remember my advice, kid. You want to get to know Miss Cartwright, you have to work for it."

"What if she doesn't want me?"

C.J. shrugged. "Change her mind. Figure out some way to make her want you." He leaned closer. "All's fair in love and war."

"You really think I can?"

The older man tossed his empty bottle toward the trashcan, hitting the center dead-on. "I think there comes a point in your life when you just have to go after what you want and damn the consequences." He stood up, clapping Tony on the shoulder, then leaned over, close to his ear. "Take it from one who knows— it's better to learn that lesson when you're young. Less catching up to do."

Tony leaned back to catch C.J.'s eye, but the pilot had already slipped his glasses back on, the mirrored frames making it impossible to read his expression. He nodded at Tony, then headed off, his last words, *think about it*, hanging in the air.

Tony did. He thought about it a lot as he watched Kyra fumble at trying to learn how to play water volleyball, her face lit with laughter. They could be friends; he'd seen it in her eyes. But never in a million years would a woman—any woman—be interested in broken, scarred Tony Moretti as a lover. Not even a woman as special as Kyra.

But her mysterious Michael...

That was a different story.

He stroked his chin as a wild, decadent, impossible thought flashed through his mind.

Maybe, just maybe, Tony Moretti and Kyra could be friends, even while she and Michael became lovers.

KYRA WALKED along the beach, kicking up the warm surf with her bare feet. She held the cell phone against her ear and waited for Mona to say something, and waited...and waited.

Frustrated, she held the phone out and stared at it. The little red light was flashing, so she must still have a connection. "Mona? Mona, for crying out loud, where'd you go?"

More silence. Then, "Are you insane?"

That was more like it. In the five years they'd been friends, Kyra'd never once known the disc jockey to be speechless. Personality-wise they had nothing in common. Mona was bold and brassy, whereas Kyra was just Kyra. They shouldn't have been friends. It defied logic. But somehow, they meshed together perfectly, and over the years, Kyra had come to depend on Mona like no one before.

"Maybe I have gone crazy," she said. "I don't know. That's why I called. You need to tell me the right thing to do."

"The right thing? You call and wake me up—"

"It's after noon."

"—and tell me that some incredible fantasy hunk was just dropped in your lap, but you *didn't* sleep with him? Kyra, that's not the right thing. That's the insane thing."

"I'm being reasonable and responsible." Kyra stopped and wiggled her toes, digging tiny holes into the sand. The truth was she'd come to Intimate Fantasy to escape *reasonable* and *responsible.* But damned if those shackles weren't tighter than she'd expected. If she couldn't convince herself, maybe Mona could.

"You're being a chicken."

"I know." She pressed her lips together. "He makes me feel...wonderful, and it terrifies me. How can I just walk away at the end if I feel like this?"

"I'm not seeing the problem," Mona said. "Did this Michael guy ask you to marry him?"

"Don't be silly."

Mona sighed, and Kyra pictured her rolling her eyes. "You want to be pragmatic? Fine. We'll do this the Kyra Cartwright analytical way, okay?"

Kyra stifled a grin. "Fine." She sat down on the beach, the phone tucked between her ear and her shoulder so she could draw random patterns in the wet sand.

"One, you paid a ton of money for this fantasy. To let it pass by would be fiscally irresponsible."

She couldn't help it. Kyra laughed. Mona was the

last person in the world to talk about financial responsibility. Still, she supposed her friend had a point—a little one, but still a point.

"Second, you went to this island to have a wild adventure. Sex and sun. The perfect island vacation. You wanted to get away from four walls and a paper-cluttered desk and into something to get your adrenaline pumping and your other juices flowing. Right?"

Her cheeks warmed, but she couldn't deny it. "Right."

"Three, you've never had a down-and-dirty, heart-pounding, loins-throbbing kind of affair."

"Loins?"

"Just work with me, okay?" Kyra imagined Mona tapping her foot, her eyebrows raised.

"Fine. Whatever. So far in my life, my loins have been calm. No throbbing. Not even a quiver." At least not until she'd met Michael.

"Well, there you go."

"There I go what?" Kyra tossed out a handful of sand in frustration.

"Into his arms. Maybe some people could have a fling without feeling any deep-down, loin-quivering attraction, but not you. This Mary person is good."

"Merrilee," Kyra corrected absently.

"Whatever. My point is this is perfect. You're completely attracted to the guy, and yet you have to walk away at the end. These Fantasies, Inc. folks didn't throw your money down the tubes. Maybe I'll come there one of these days."

"But the walking away part? I told you. He makes me feel all—"

"It doesn't matter," Mona said. "Because you don't know who he is. Repeat after me—a-non-y-mous. You can walk away from this guy 'cause there is no guy at the other end. No one you know, anyway. Didn't you say you're not even sure Michael's his real name?"

"Well, yeah." Danielle had told her the staff was clueless, and there was no registered guest named Michael. Even if it was a total lie, it didn't help Kyra. "I don't know..."

"Knock it off. I know you better than that. You want this guy. And you knew damn well I'd tell you to go for it."

She closed her eyes, blocking out the truth. "I feel guilty wanting it."

"Come on. I mean, I believe that you feel guilty, but that's just silly. You paid a ton of money for this vacation, and you deserve to get every penny's worth. Besides, you're the most responsible person I know. You've kept your family together, along with the business. You're going to agree to marry Harold—"

"Which you don't approve of."

"No, I don't. But it is the Kyra-esque thing to do. I've given up trying to talk you out of it. But in the meantime, have a little fun. That's what you paid for, right?"

"I suppose."

"And like I've been saying all along—anonymous sex with the perfect man? *That*, my dear, is one hell of a fantasy."

TONY LAY on the bed, an ice pack tucked under his lower back as he stared at the ceiling and tried to decide what to do. He wanted to go to her, but feared that she'd turn away from him again.

Of course, turning away from Michael wasn't the same as turning away from Tony. She wouldn't be walking away from a useless and broken man, just a man she didn't know. He'd be disappointed, true, but he wouldn't be crushed.

Go for it.

A little voice kept repeating the phrase. Take a risk. Take a chance. He knew she was attracted to him, just as he was to her. And he had less than a week left on this island. When in his life would such an opportunity ever arise again? When would he ever have another chance with a woman who made his blood burn—and who wanted him as badly as he wanted her?

A sharp knock at the door distracted him, and for half a second he entertained the fantasy that Kyra was outside waiting on the front porch, ready to throw herself into his arms.

He rolled his eyes at his own foolishness. In less than twenty-four hours, he'd become completely infatuated with the woman. It was absurd. Even if they did start something, in the end, he'd only get hurt. They'd part ways at the end of their week, never to see each other again. Or, worse, she'd discover his secret and simply walk away, the disgust on her face only mildly camouflaged.

Again, the knock. Louder this time.

With a groan, he sat up, one hand automatically reaching behind him to soothe the sore muscles. "Come in."

The door pushed open, and Stuart stepped in. Relief and disappointment swept through Tony.

"Hey, guy," Stuart said. "I'm going around telling all the guests that it looks like we've got another storm coming through tonight."

"Right. I know. Sounds like it's going to spoil the beach party." For the past several days, Tony had noticed the flyers for the Beach Blanket Bingo Party on the west beach. Tony hadn't intended to go, but Michael had. If not to the actual party, at least to hang around the periphery and make sure nothing untoward happened to anyone.

Stuart shrugged. "The ETA's not until two in the morning. Merrilee called from the mainland and said that so long as we had enough Jeeps and drivers to get the guests back to their cabanas if it blew in early, we could go ahead with it." His eyes darted around the cabana. "Are you gonna make it?"

"Not sure. Maybe." He thought of Kyra, wondering if she'd be there.

"You should come."

"*I should?*"

Stuart flushed slightly, then turned toward the dresser and focused on the black eye patch that sat in front of the mirror. "Yeah, you should." He turned, heading for the door, then stopped at the threshold, turning around with a smug expression. "And in case you didn't realize, the party's just a few yards from Kyra's cabana. She said she'd definitely be there tonight."

MERRILEE AND her staff knew how to put on a bash. From the front of her cabana, Kyra looked around the bonfire-lit beach, hugging herself. It was quite a party.

By the time the evening was over, Kyra hoped it would be a private party. She had no reason to think he'd come to her, not after she'd walked away, but now that she'd talked herself into it, she desperately hoped he would. A bloodred heat swept through her body just from the mere thought of him. She'd probably spontaneously combust when she actually saw him.

Of course, if he didn't show up, she could always hang upside down from a tree. *That* would get his attention.

She smiled to herself. Mona would probably suggest she hang upside down in a dress with no underwear. Not a chance. Bold, Kyra could handle. Bold *and* brazen, no.

Barefoot, she stepped off the porch into the cool sand, feeling decadent and alive. Just like in her professional life, she'd made a decision, she'd pushed every doubt out of her mind. She had a plan to seduce Michael, and she was going after it with both barrels. In fact, now that she'd made the decision, it seemed so much the obvious route that she wondered why she'd ever hesitated.

Because you're a chicken.

Well, that was true enough, but her afternoon of windsurfing lessons had cemented her decision. The instructor had been so absorbed with safety and theory that they never even got off the beach. If Kyra wanted adventure, she was going to have to take steps. And she intended to step in Michael's direction.

Considering the storm that was supposed to blow in later, the night air was remarkably still. A short distance from her cabana, a fifties-style band was cranking out "Rock Around The Clock," and she strolled in that direction, approaching the largest of the three bonfires.

She found C.J. and Stuart near the grill. C.J. was wearing a ridiculous-looking chef's hat, and Stuart was snarfing down hot dogs as fast as C.J. could roll them off the grill.

"I feel like I should have worn a poodle skirt." Kyra had to shout to be heard over the band.

"Great, isn't it?" Stuart asked. "Want to dance?"

Kyra shook her head. "I'm starving. You go ahead. I'm going to hit C.J. up for a hot dog."

Stuart nodded, then bopped away, throwing his arm

around one of the college girls who waitressed at the restaurant. Soon, they'd melded into the crowd jamming in front of the band.

"What's your pleasure?" C.J. asked.

"Mustard, ketchup, relish, chili and onions—wait, hold the onions," she quickly corrected.

He shot her a sly look and she felt her cheeks flush. She glanced around the beach, looking to change the subject. "Seems like everyone on the island turned out."

"Pretty much. I don't see Tony, though."

"Tony?" She tried to place the name, then remembered. "The guy from the pool. He seemed nice. Why wouldn't he come?" She grinned. "Does he have a romantic fantasy going on this evening?"

C.J. added some hot dogs to the fire. "I can only hope. But no. More likely he's self-conscious."

She remembered his reaction when they'd met and the way he'd turned away, angling to keep his face in the shade. "His scar?"

"From what I understand it's fairly new."

She nodded slowly. "It must be difficult, seeing your face change overnight like that. But scar or no, I think he's good-looking." She remembered his broad shoulders and wide smile, wondering at the sanity of any woman who'd turn away simply because his eye was ringed by such a nasty scar. Then again, a lot of women put stock in that sort of thing. "He's got a rugged, protective look. There must be a lot of women who still go ga-ga over him." He seemed like a genuinely nice guy, and she hoped it was true.

"You included?"

"I'm not the ga-ga type." Her cheeks warmed with the lie. The truth was she wasn't *usually* the ga-ga type. But Michael had changed all that. She smiled at C.J. "I'm the practical type."

He passed her a hot dog loaded down with all the trimmings except onions. "Well, now, that's too bad. Especially on an island like this, sometimes it's downright fun to fall hard and fast."

Kyra wasn't about to admit that she may have done that very thing, so she took a huge bite and chewed furiously.

"My dear, will you watch the grill for a second?" C.J.'s voice sounded unusually strained. "I need to...uh...go get some more buns."

He pulled off his apron and left without waiting for her agreement. Kyra stood there, perplexed, even more so when she looked down and saw a box with enough buns to feed a small country. She glanced in the direction he'd gone, but he'd blended into the dark. Odd.

The wind kicked up, sending a firestorm of sparks shooting up into the air. Past the bonfire, Merrilee and Danielle were making their way toward the grill. Kyra waved to them.

"Did we put you on the payroll?" Merrilee joked. "Why aren't you out dancing with the other guests?"

"Oh. I...um..." Kyra frowned. "I'm just watching it

for a sec. Dog?" She stabbed a hot dog with the serving fork and held it out.

"Thanks," Danielle said, grabbing a bun. "Who're you taking over for?"

"C.J.," Kyra said, hoping she wasn't getting the pilot in trouble. "He...uh...had to go get something."

Merrilee sighed. "I keep missing that man."

"Pardon?"

The older woman smiled. "It's nothing important. He's just our newest employee, and every time I make a point to meet him, we manage somehow to completely miss each other." She laughed, but the sound didn't quite reach her eyes.

After a moment, she smiled at Kyra. "At any rate, I'm glad you're here. I was hoping we could chat a bit about how you're enjoying your stay so far. Danielle said you were looking for me earlier."

"Yes, I was."

"Danielle, do you mind?" Merrilee looked pointedly at the grill.

"Not at all." The girl took the serving fork from Kyra and donned the apron C.J. had left behind.

Kyra and Merrilee headed toward the water, walking just shy of the breaking waves. "So, what did you want to see me about?"

Kyra kicked at the sand with her toes. "Nothing important. Not anymore."

"The problem resolved itself?"

"You could say that." She drew in a breath, gathering her courage. "I chickened out. I didn't seize it...him...my fantasy." She pressed her lips together, wondering if she'd disappointed the older woman. "But now I've bucked up my courage." She stooped to pick up an intricate shell, then traced her finger along the spiraling pattern. "I'm sorry."

"Sorry? Nonsense." Merrilee took her hand, gave it a gentle squeeze. "You needed time. There's no shame in that."

"I just hope I see him again. That I didn't ruin everything by not taking the fantasy when it was offered." She searched Merrilee's face, but found no clues. Blinking, she tried to bolster her courage. "At any rate, I've had a long time to think about it, and I'm ready now."

"Bravo, Kyra. It sounds like the island is working its magic on you."

"Magic?"

"Certainly. I like to think that none of my guests leaves one of the Fantasies resorts without a new perspective on life. And isn't that a bit like magic?"

Kyra had to agree. If anyone could spin a little magic, Merrilee could.

"Danielle and I just arrived back on the island, and we need to go get ready for tomorrow. You have fun at the party." She moved away, heading back up the beach toward the lights from the bonfire. After a moment, she stopped and turned again. "Oh, and Kyra? I wouldn't worry if I were you. I imagine that you'll see Michael again tonight."

Waves of relief washed over her, and she stood there like a fool with a big, goofy smile as Merrilee faded into the night. "When I find you, Michael," she whispered happily, "you're mine for the week."

"I'm glad to hear that."

She jumped and yelped, then whirled around to face him. "You scared me to death." Her heart pounded furiously in her chest, but whether from fear or desire, she wasn't sure.

"Sorry." He moved closer, his one vivid green eye fixed on her, a lock of roguish black hair curling across his forehead from under his cap. His chin and jawline were covered with a thick evening beard. Like her father, he seemed the type who needed to shave at least twice a day, and the dark shadow made him seem more rugged, more sexy.

She inhaled, her breath shaky.

He combed his fingers through her loose hair, the pressure of his hand on the back of her head pulling her to him until she was close enough that she could smell his scent. It was familiar, something she'd smelled recently, and she frowned for a moment before placing it. Obsession for Men.

She giggled.

"What?"

"Your cologne."

"You don't like it?"

"I love it. It's just that I picture you lurking in shad-

ows and fog, not buying cologne under harsh department store lights."

"And I picture you in candlelight."

"You do?" Her voice sounded squeaky, and she
cringed.

He leaned forward, his mouth near her ear. "Naked
in the candlelight." Barely a whisper, his words stirred
her. Her knees went weak, her body liquid.

As if he knew her most intimate thoughts, he curved
his arm around her waist, supporting her. "Tell me
you want me, too, Kyra. Tell me you want me and
make my fantasy come true."

His fantasy?

She tilted her head back, wanting to read the truth in
his eyes. Could she of all people really be the object of
someone's fantasy? The thought had never even occurred to her and she found the possibility to be flatter-
ing, even exciting.

But she wasn't at all sure it was true. She wasn't even
entirely certain he was a guest, and not staff, on the island.

Still, when she looked into his eye, when she
watched the expression dance on the shadows covering his face, she saw only desire reflected there. Desire
so intense, that her breath actually caught in her throat.

"Kyra?"

She nodded, mute, then fought to find her voice.

"Yes," she finally said. "Yes, I want you, too."

5

SHE WANTED HIM. She honestly wanted him, and that made Tony feel like the tallest, strongest man on the planet.

Of course, she didn't actually know who he was. Not really. She'd fallen for an illusion, his secret identity, the man out to protect the island guests from boogeymen and the pitfalls of nature. But the real Tony? Well, his white knight days were long over.

Still, the thought of Kyra in his arms, in his bed, whatever the terms...well, the image was enticing, and not one he intended to turn away. He'd told the truth—in a lot of ways, she was his fantasy. A woman who looked at him like he was the whole world. A woman who wanted him and wasn't afraid to show it. A woman who could make him forget, even if only for the night, just who he really was.

Alan was right. He did need a woman. A woman like Krya who didn't know—wouldn't ever know—his secrets.

"Your place or mine?" she said. Despite the flirtatious tone, he heard a quiver of nerves, and her hesitancy only increased his desire. Somehow, she'd fallen for him. In some small way, she belonged to him.

The realization humbled him. She was sharing so much with him, trusting so much to him. He held out his hand for her to take, squeezing her fingers lightly as he curled his hand around hers.

"Yours," he said, taking care to remember to keep his voice pitched low. "It's closer." And since he shared his place with his alter ego, it was out of the question.

He pulled her closer, automatically moving to her left side so that he could see her out of his uncovered eye.

"We'll miss the party," she said, looking back over her shoulder.

He felt like a heel. Of course she'd probably come to Intimate Fantasy expecting to meet some man who'd sweep her off her feet. A man who'd take her out dancing and for long walks along the beach. A man who knew his way around a classy menu. The last thing in the world she'd probably expected was to be paired with some mysterious man in black who came and went with the night, keeping to the shadows and as far away from crowds as possible.

"Do you want to go back?" he asked, unsure what he'd do if she said yes. He could always wait in her cabana. Joining the festivities was simply out of the question.

"No!" Her response was quick and adamant, and relief surged through him. "I mean, not unless you do."

"I'm not interested in anyone at the party. I'm only interested in you."

She met his eyes. "Naked and in candlelight, right?" she asked boldly.

He grinned, enjoying her playfulness. "Well, we can always blow out the candle."

"Just so long as we're clear on the naked part."

"Oh, I think we're clear." As fabulous as she looked in the sarong-style skirt and flower-print bikini top, he would be even happier to see her out of it.

They were almost to her cabana when she stopped, turning around to face him. The lights from her cabin lit her hair in silhouette, giving her an ethereal appearance. "That goes for you, too," his angel said.

"What's that?"

"Naked."

He let his gaze roam up her body. "Sweetheart, I wouldn't have it any other way."

"Except..." She swallowed, her hands balled into fists.

"What?" he asked. "What's wrong?"

She took a deep breath and looked him in the eye. "Except for the patch." She licked her lips, then dropped her gaze. "I don't want you to take off the patch. And no lights. Nothing but candlelight, anyway."

"All right." Since he had no intention of letting her get a good look at him, her condition was an easy one.

She looked up, her head cocked. "That's okay? You don't mind?"

"I wouldn't have it any other way," he said.

He could tell the moment understanding struck her.

"You want me," she said, "but you don't want me to know who you are."

He shrugged. "Clever girl."

He could practically see the inevitable question pass over her face. Why not? But she didn't ask it. She didn't pry.

He, however, wasn't nearly so polite. "You want me to stay anonymous," he said simply.

She nodded.

"Why?"

"Isn't it obvious?"

Not to him. "Tell me."

She slipped closer, sliding her arms around his neck, her face close to his. "Because, darling Michael, that's part of my fantasy."

BEFORE SHE COULD talk herself out of it, she captured his mouth with her own, thrilled that she could be so bold and reckless. He tasted like sin—decadent, delicious, more satisfying than chocolate—and she reveled in it, exploring, tasting, teasing.

Her head was light, her knees weak—every cliché she'd ever heard about hit her in the overwhelming onslaught of pure passion. It was all right there, in her head, her belly, between her thighs.

He nibbled on her lower lip, teasing her with his teeth as shots of electricity scattered through her. Her body melded to his like molten steel, and she pressed against him, centering his thigh between hers in the futile hope that the pressure might somehow squelch the craving fast building inside her.

His hands caressed her back, his fingers splayed across her skin while his thumbs stroked her side and teased the swell of her breasts. She moved against him, silently trying to urge his hands forward, wanting his hands hard on her, wanting the storm inside her to build to a maelstrom, desperate for him to take her right then, right there, so there could be no chance that she'd do something as foolish as change her mind.

"Please," she murmured, surprised she could even form sounds, "touch me."

"I am touching you."

His voice, raw and gravelly, seemed to pool between her thighs. She realized his hand had slipped between them, and he was stroking her through the thin material of her wrap-around skirt.

"Tell me what you want," he whispered.

More. She mouthed the word, but couldn't say it out loud. She was being decadent. Wild and wanton. And damned if that didn't scare her to death.

She'd never behaved like this before, never asked for what she wanted. Never *wanted* like she did now. Not like she felt with him. A wave of fear crested, decades of being the good girl kept pulling her back until she felt herself stiffen in his arms.

His hands stroked her hair, soothing and calming her. "Whatever you want, sweetheart. As slow as you want."

His finger slipped under her chin, tilted her head up, and she saw the concern on his face. He took a tiny step back, still holding her hand, but increasing the distance between them. Whereas before they had almost seemed like one person, now there was a thin strip of air. A billion molecules keeping her from him, and to Kyra, the gap seemed wider than the Grand Canyon.

He turned slightly and nodded toward the ocean. "Why don't we backtrack a little? Take a walk on the beach? I can tell you bad jokes, and you can pretend they're funny."

He took a step, but she tugged him back. "No!" She gnawed on her lower lip as he stopped and looked at her, the corner of his mouth twitching.

"I promise the jokes aren't that bad."

She laughed, thankful he could so easily put her at ease. "I don't want to talk." She shook her head, frustrated. "That's not what I meant. Talking is great. You're great. I just don't want to talk now. I didn't mean...earlier...it wasn't—"

He hushed her with a gentle finger to her lips. "I want you more than any woman I've wanted in a long,

long time. If you're telling me that you want to go inside your cabana with me, then just nod."

She kissed the tip of his finger, then, before she lost her tenuous courage, she took it in her mouth, swirling her tongue around the digit, relishing the salty taste of his skin. She closed her eyes and drew his finger in further, letting her teeth graze his knuckles as she abandoned herself to passion.

He moaned, and his free hand slipped around her waist, pulling her close until she couldn't mistake just how much he wanted her. His breath was hot against her ear, stirring her hair as a sound of pure masculine satisfaction escaped him.

"Sweetheart, that damn well better be a yes, because I don't think I can stand it if that's your way of letting a guy down gently."

With one final sultry tug of her mouth, she released his finger. "Yes," she said, hooking one arm around his neck. "That most definitely is a yes."

With unfamiliar boldness, she urged him closer until their lips touched. The contact was gentle, but the effect was anything but. As if taking its cue from her reaction, the wind kicked up.

"The storm's coming," he whispered, his lips moving against hers.

"We should go inside." She tilted her head back and smiled at him. "Quickly, before I change my mind."

He twisted a finger in one wind-tossed strand of her hair. "Is that something you're likely to do?"

"What do you think?"

"I think it's time to go inside. Because I don't intend to let you get away."

HE WATCHED as she fumbled with the key, finally managing to open the door. "Sorry. Just a little nervous." She stepped over the threshold and stood awkwardly. "Well, this is it. My little home away from home."

She kept the lights off, but from the dim light of the moon he could see that her cabana was sparsely but comfortably furnished—a bed, a small couch, a cozy breakfast area. With its abundance of windows and bright-colored furniture, the room was airy and inviting.

"I like what you've done with the place," he said lightly. He knew she was nervous, clearly not a woman prone to casual affairs, and it humbled him that she so obviously wanted him.

She headed for the kitchen area and started opening drawers. "Yeah, I spent hours choosing a theme. I almost went with Feng Shui, but decided on island casual instead." She shut the last drawer and shrugged. "No candles."

"In my cabana, they're under the sink in the bathroom with the hurricane supplies."

"Your cabana?" she asked from the bathroom. She came out holding two thick candles. "Ta-da. So I guess that means you're a guest here, too."

"Some of the staff have cabanas. Only the summer kids stay in the bunk room."

Her mouth twitched. "Not exactly an answer, but the best I'm going to get, right?"

"Right." He took the candles and matches from her, letting his fingers graze hers. "Not to be presumptuous, but why don't we light one by the bed?"

"Um. Sure. Bed. Fine."

Grinning, he moved to the bedside table and lit a single candle, filling the area with a flickering orange glow.

"Much more romantic, don't you think?" He was forcing himself to make small talk when all he wanted to do was lose himself inside her. Her nearness was driving him nuts, but she was nervous, and for her he was going to take it slowly, was going to make it perfect.

"Very romantic." She moved closer, standing just a few inches from him.

Her skin glowed in the soft light, begging for his touch, and he traced the line of her neck and shoulder with the tip of his finger. "They sell candles in the gift shop," he said, sure he sounded like an idiot, but her presence was turning his mind to mush. "I'll get some for tomorrow."

Her eyes danced with mischief. "Oh? So you figure you'll be back tomorrow night?"

He blinked, suddenly realizing that for her this might be a one-time fling. "Oh. Well...I...actually—"

"Michael?"

"Yes?"

She took a deep breath, then reached behind her back and unfastened her halter. "I'm not nervous anymore." She concentrated on the knot at her neck, and he watched, mesmerized, as the top fell to the ground.

She was stunning, and he could have stared at her for hours if she'd let him.

"Touch me," she whispered, moving into his arms.

He couldn't remember ever being happier to oblige a request. Her breasts were firm and fit perfectly into the cups of his hands. He flicked his thumb over her erect nipple, felt himself harden as she gasped and tilted her head back, exposing the sleek line of her neck.

He could see her pulse beat in her neck, and he bent to kiss her there, the warmth of her skin against his lips tantalizing. With deliberate slowness, he trailed his kisses lower, each soft moan nearly driving him over the edge. Her breath came in staccato bursts, and when he closed his mouth around her breast, she cried out, only to stifle the sound with her fist.

He wanted more, needed more. Her pure, honest reactions were the most potent of aphrodisiacs, and he craved her. Wanted to explore—to taste—every inch of her.

"Kiss me."

The demand was little more than a whisper, but he obliged, closing his mouth hard over hers, trying to convey without words how much he wanted her and how much this night meant to him.

While his tongue danced with hers, his hands skimmed down her body, then back up, grazing the soft skin around her waist, her belly, then kneading her breasts. Gently at first, then rougher as she broke their kiss, urging him on with soft pleas of "more, yes, more."

"You're delicious," he murmured, then trailed his tongue from her navel to her nipple just to prove the point.

"Oh, Michael." He noticed with pure masculine delight the quiver in her voice. "My knees are weak. The bed?"

He shook his head and pulled himself up. "Not yet." It had been almost a year since he'd been with a woman, and he wasn't sure if he could hold back if they were in bed, with her warm and willing under him. But he wanted to maintain control of himself for as long as possible. Wanted the night to last forever. Wanted to take her to the edge and have her desperate for more. For him.

Gently, he urged them backward until her back was pressed against the wall. Then he urged her hands up over her head.

"But I want to touch you."

He shook his head. "Later. I promise. Right now, just close your eyes."

Her smile—a combination of pure feminine power

and complete trust—just about did him in. When she obliged, he gently kissed each lid before trailing his fingers down to the knot at her hip.

One simple little knot held her entire skirt on, and naturally it tormented him with its stubbornness. He considered simply pushing the skirt up around her waist, but he wanted to see all of her, every inch. And that meant loosing the damn knot.

"Need a hand?" Barely a whisper, her amused voice drifted over him.

"I've got it." He'd spent every summer of his life before the accident on a sailboat. He knew knots. So it was particularly frustrating that one simple square knot refused to cooperate. Of course, on a boat, he wasn't delirious from lust.

When he managed to untie it, though, he knew his effort had been worth it. The skirt fell away, pooling on the tile floor at her bare feet. She shifted, pressing her legs together, and he grinned, amused by her attempts at modesty.

With something close to reverence, he traced the outline of her panties. When he cupped his hand over the dark vee, she moaned and arched her back, spreading her legs for him. Stifling a groan, he stroked her through the soft silk that was already damp with the evidence of her desire.

His erection strained painfully against the confines of his jeans, and he shifted to ease the pressure, not wanting to take his hands from her body even long enough to undo his fly.

Slowly, he moved closer, his lips to her cheek, his body against hers. She whimpered, the small sound sending his blood coursing hot through his body. But when she moved her arms down to stroke his hair, he pulled back gently, taking her hands between his own.

"Not yet. Just you. Trust me."

She nodded as he urged her hands back up the wall. Her body was lithe and firm. Stretched out like that she seemed to offer him an invitation to touch, to explore, and he happily accepted the offer. He kissed her ear, teasing the soft curve, then trailed kisses down her throat, her shoulder, and lower still.

He took her breast in his mouth, tasting, sucking, as his hand trailed lower. Her skin was soft under his fingers, and when he reached the elastic band of her panties, he didn't stop. He slipped his finger under and stroked the coarse, short hair, and she gasped, sucking in air and tilting her head back.

He teased her nipple with his teeth, and she moved her hips under his hand, urging him lower and lower until his fingers found her slick, sweet center. She was wet and hot and ready, and it thrilled him more than he could have imagined to know that she was ready for him. That she wanted *him*.

Taking care to taste every inch of her, he nibbled his way down, flicking his tongue over the curve of her breast, tasting the salt of her skin, dipping his tongue into her belly button.

She laughed softly. "That tickles." Then, "Please, I want to touch you."

"Soon," he promised.

He knelt slowly, slipping his hands under either side of her panties and dragging them down over her hips. She made another soft noise as they fell to the floor and he urged her legs apart. He felt his back tighten painfully as he urged her closer, but he ignored it, not willing to let anything spoil the moment, wanting only to kneel before her, to breathe in her feminine scent, to taste every single inch of her.

Slipping his hands behind her, he cupped her rear and dipped his head. He wanted to kiss the inside of her thigh, that soft place that drove women wild. And Kyra was no exception. She trembled under his touch, dropping her hands to his head. This time, he didn't object.

He moved his kisses higher, drunk from the taste of her. And when she knocked his cap off and buried her fingers in his hair, he did the same, burying his tongue deep in her, then teasing her secret feminine places with the tip of his tongue. She writhed under him, her fingers knotting in his hair. A spasm shot through his back, and he pulled her closer, riding out the pain.

"Michael." Her voice was hoarse, unsteady, and filled with passion. For a fleeting moment, a twinge of sadness caught him. He'd give anything to hear his real name on her lips, but that wasn't possible, and for now—for her—he'd take what he could.

"Please," she said, cupping his face with her hands, and urging him to look at her, with her eyes glazed from passion. "I want you. Inside me. Now."

It was, of course, a demand he wouldn't think of refusing. But with his back screaming in pain, he didn't know how the hell he could accept.

6

HE MOVED UP the wall, ignoring the pain in his lower back as he straightened. Every cell in his body hummed, and he longed to bury himself in her, to give them both what they craved.

"Please," she repeated. "Now."

"Soon," he whispered.

"You promised me naked," she murmured, her breath hot against his ear. She reached for his jeans, fumbled with his fly, then slid her hands under the denim, urging his jeans down. "I like a man who keeps his promises."

And he wanted to keep every one of them—both spoken and unspoken. He took an involuntary step toward her and realized his legs were caught in the circle of denim around his ankles. "I think you've trapped me."

"Good." She caught the collar of his T-shirt and pulled him forward, then planted a mind-blowing kiss on him. Apparently, his sweet Kyra had decided she wanted to call the shots, and he was more than happy to succumb to her whims.

With a tug, she lifted his shirt. Suddenly her hands

were on his waist, soft and warm. She inched her fingers up, pushing the shirt up even as she lowered herself to trail kisses on his now-exposed skin.

He tried to reach for her, but his hands were caught in the sleeves of his shirt above his head. As he fumbled, she pressed closer, her breasts soft against his chest. He tossed the shirt aside, his breath coming hard and ragged, wanting nothing more than to take her right there against the wall until they were both sated and limp in each other's arms.

"Bed." His voice was hoarse from passion.

"Yes." She kissed the corner of his mouth. "But you're still trapped." With a devious grin, she let her hands glide down his body, down his stomach, then lower. Her fingers teased the elastic band of his briefs, and he had some idea of the pure, glorious, wonderful torment he'd put her through only moments before.

Desperate for her touch, he caught her hand under his, heard her soft gasp as he pressed their joined hands against the full length of his arousal. "I want you," he whispered.

"I feel it." Her voice was breathy. Her body, pressed close, burned hot. He longed to bury himself in that heat, to sheath himself in her, to lose himself in this glorious dream and never wake up.

She stroked him, taking him to the brink, and he moaned, a deep gutteral sound in the back of his throat.

"Are you going to let me finish?" she asked, a tease in her voice.

"I think I'll die if you don't."

She slid down further, her hands working their magic on his legs, until every single inch of him burned with desire. When she'd untied his sneakers, he slipped out of his jeans then urged her back up to face him. "Bed," he repeated. "Now."

She shook her head, a devilish smile playing across her face. "We're still not even." She snapped the band of his underwear lightly. "Naked, remember?"

He chuckled. "For you, my dear, no demand is too much."

He stepped out of his underwear and pressed against her, urging her backward until she was against the wall again. They fit together perfectly, and she spread her legs just slightly in both invitation and silent demand. He pressed closer, her slick wetness against the length of him an erotic, sensual tease, and he considered taking her right there. But he forced himself to wait, fearful his back couldn't take it.

She protested as he pulled away, breaking contact, but he took her hand and urged her to the bed. She lay on the spread, her body glowing in the candlelight, her eyes wide, but dreamy. The tableau was pure sensuality, but there was an air of innocence, too. She was everything—sweet, yet sensual; demanding, yet giving.

"Now," she urged. "I've got...you know...in the table by the bed."

He couldn't help his grin as she tugged on his hand, urging him forward. The woman was a sultry combination of shy and sexy, and it just about did him in. He followed willingly, knowing he couldn't, wouldn't, disappoint her. It seemed as if the whole world turned on losing himself inside her, and he could think of only one way to be absolutely certain that his sore back would survive the night.

He slid in next to her, propped up on his side as he stroked her hair, then moved in to capture her mouth with a kiss. Her hand trailed down, teasing and stroking, making him even harder, a thing he wouldn't have thought possible.

"Now," he said, echoing her words. He rolled on his back, urging her on top of him. "Please, sweetheart, now."

KYRA SWALLOWED. She was hardly a virgin, but she'd never been a particularly, well, aggressive lover, though that was changing a bit tonight. And now Michael seemed to want her to take the lead. She wanted to. Oh, how she wanted to.

Slowly, sensually, she moved on top of him, leaning forward to slide open the table's drawer and pull out one of the little foil packets she'd brought with her. She arched her back as she slid against his body, playing her hands down his bare chest and trailing kisses in their wake. His taste was pure male, and she wanted to sample every part of him, to gorge herself on the wonderful taste that was purely Michael.

He made her feel things she'd never felt before. Like she was spinning out of control. Like every part of her body burned with a fire she couldn't control or classify.

Alive. Every inch of her. She was alive and the feeling was pure heaven.

She moved lower, her knees pressed into the bed on either side of him. She was wide open, ready for him, and wanting him so desperately she had to fight the urge to sink herself onto him and give them both what they craved. *Not yet.*

She'd never felt so powerful, so special, and she wanted the feeling to continue just a little longer. Wanted them both on the edge so that when relief finally came she could hold on to the feeling and never, ever let it go.

"I want you, Kyra." His hands stroked her back, her bottom, urging her over him. His voice was raw, and she felt a surge of power knowing that he was on the very edge of control and that she was the one who had taken him there. She could feel the hard length of him pressed against her, ready. Ready for her. With slow, languid movements, she writhed against him, knowing that he too was at the brink.

"Oh, God, Kyra, you're driving me crazy."

She lowered her mouth to his lips, brushed a soft kiss over them. "Am I?"

"Vixen," he said, a tease in his voice. His hands

grazed her back, his skin rough against her rear. He cupped her bottom and she moved forward, desperate to let him touch her there, everywhere.

She moaned, deep and needy when his finger slipped inside her, and she pressed against him, wanting him deeper, wanting more of him, all of him.

"Payback, sweetheart," he said, tormenting her by taking his finger away.

She met his eye, saw the same passion reflected there that burned through her. With a silent prayer that she wouldn't fumble and destroy the mood, she got the little packet open and managed to sheath him.

"Now. Oh, yes, please. Now."

Arching her back, she lifted herself, then moved down, impaling herself on the length of him. She gasped as he filled her, body and soul. He reached up, his hands stroking her breasts, fondling rock-hard nipples, and she swallowed a moan.

She rocked against him, needing everything he could give. Through a haze of passion, she felt one of his hands slip down, grazing the skin of her belly, leaving a trail of hot, hyperaware flesh. He moved lower and lower still, then slipped his hand between their joined bodies.

"You're so slick," he murmured. "You feel wonderful. Kiss me."

She complied readily, bending forward, increasing the pressure of him inside her and stroking her. He seemed to be touching her everywhere, and she closed her mouth hungrily over his, as joined as two people could possibly be.

They stayed that way, moving against each other, colors swirling around her while the wind outside the cabana howled, the storm building even as the pressure inside her built. Faster and faster, tighter and tighter, she tried to hang on, tried to make it last, but in the end, she had to let herself go, and she arched back, holding on to his waist as the world exploded around them in a fit of colors and stars.

She drew in a breath. "Wow."

His smile was gentle, and he reached up to stroke her face. "I'd say that pretty much covers it. Come here."

He urged her lower until she was curled up next to him, their bodies slick from the sweat of lovemaking. He stroked her side, sending little shockwaves ricocheting through her.

"You better be careful. I might have to jump you again," she teased.

"Is that a promise?" He kissed her nose, then pulled her closer.

"Maybe it is." She shifted against him, wanting every part of her to be touching some part of him.

"How did I get so lucky?" he asked, his voice sleepy.

"Lucky?"

"To find you."

"Oh." No one had ever made her feel so important, so special, and her eyes welled. She blinked, frustrated.

"I guess I just like my men heroic," she said lightly. "Rescue me from a tree, and I'm yours."

"So that's the trick," he said.

She thought she caught a hint of sadness in his voice, but she dismissed it as a product of her own, overemotional state. She'd done the right thing, gathering up her courage for this sensual adventure. She was sure of it. They meshed somehow, his lightest touch waking every part of her body.

But even more than the pure, simple thrill of his touch, the truth was, he'd struck a nerve. Touched some part of her she hadn't expected. He made her feel desirable and feminine. He actually wanted her—not because of her family, not because of her company, not even because everyone expected it. He'd simply seen her and wanted her. And, heaven help her, she'd wanted him right back.

It couldn't be permanent. She knew that, though she wanted to pretend it would last forever. She already had something permanent waiting for her in Dallas. Permanent, responsible. The life she was born to. The responsibilities she couldn't escape.

She'd have Michael for the week. She'd have his memory for the rest of her life.

KYRA'S BODY curled against his, soft and warm. She was one special lady. An enchantress. How else could he have felt like himself again? Hell, she'd taken him to the edge and over, working on him like a drug, making him forget the pain in his back, turning the pain into a haze of need, of desire.

He stroked her cheek, and she stirred slightly, her lips parted in sleep. Carefully, so he wouldn't wake her, he scooted to the edge of the bed.

Being in her arms may have been therapeutic, but now he was paying the price. Lightning flashed as the storm raged outside, and he fumbled for the matches, then relit the single candle they'd blown out earlier. Moving slowly, he slipped out of bed and headed for her kitchenette to search for ice for his back.

He emptied a few cubes into a dishtowel, then held the makeshift pack in place as he wandered around her cabana aimlessly, trying to loosen up. The difference in their rooms was obvious. Not so much the style, but the occupant.

Where he was a total slob, she was neat. Already, his was decorated in early-American laundry, while her clothes hung neatly in the half-open closet, not one piece of dirty clothing on the floor, except what they'd left last night.

Her dresser was topped with a brush, a little jar, a bottle of spray, and a notepad open to a page of neatly printed lists. He resisted the urge to read her notes, but gave in to the urge to smell the spray—strawberry.

Her bathroom fit the pattern. Hell, even her towels were folded neatly on the bar, and there wasn't one glob of toothpaste in the sink.

On the table next to the front door, he found a room-service card and noticed that she'd put in a standing order for breakfast. He grinned. He was lucky if he remembered to hang out the card in time to order coffee for the next morning. So far, he'd remembered once. Every other day, he'd had to make his own from the supply in the well-stocked kitchenette. Since culinary skills weren't among his repertoire, so far the stuff hadn't been drinkable, and he'd become a late-morning fixture at the poolside restaurant.

Thinking about his morning routine reminded him that he needed to be gone by sun-up. They'd made love in the light of only one candle, and he didn't want to risk her getting a better look at his face if the storm broke and the sun came out.

Though a tiny part of him wanted to wake her up and tell her everything—wanted her to cover his face with kisses and tell him it didn't matter—he knew that was only a fantasy. He glanced at the clock. Four forty-five. About an hour until the sun started its slow rise over the ocean.

He longed to take her outside, to hold her hand as they watched the sun's spectacle. But even if the storm stopped raging, he couldn't be with her in the light.

He glanced toward the bed and saw that she'd kicked the sheet off. Her skin glowed in the reflected light of the candle, and he felt his body tighten.

He moved toward her quietly, careful not to wake her when he slipped the candle back onto the table and dropped the ice-filled towel onto the floor. Taking care not to shake the bed, he slid in next to her and blew out the candle.

His back still ached, but it was a different kind of ache that urged him on now. And though he would pay the price later, he had to have her again. He was rock hard just from looking at her, and he needed to lose himself in her slick heat.

Gently, he kissed her cheek, then the corner of her mouth. She turned, rolling onto her back, mumbling soft words through the blanket of sleep. He stayed still, not wanting her to awaken just yet. She was dreaming, and he wanted her to dream of him.

One arm was over her head, and her legs were spread. He knelt over her, dipping his head to taste her breast. She sighed, and his heart constricted when he realized that she'd whispered his name. In sleep, her hand drifted down, resting against her cheek. Her other hand idly stroked her side, and he kissed each finger in turn, stopping to concentrate on her index finger.

He drew it into his mouth, relishing the taste of her. With his tongue, he teased her finger, his own eyes closed, urging her to the very brink of wakefulness.

She stretched beneath him, making soft sounds that drove him crazy. She spread her legs wider, and he took that as an invitation. With his fingers, he explored her wet heat, dipping into her core, feeling her tighten around him.

"Yes," she murmured, her hips shifting, drawing him in more. "Oh, yes."

Even in sleep, she wanted him.

The knowledge filled him, made him harder. He rubbed himself against the soft skin of her thigh, teasing and torturing them both.

Her eyes were still closed, her mouth curled up. She looked beautiful, ethereal, and he wanted her.

She whispered his name, and the sound of his name on her lips brought him to the brink. He thrust inside her then, and her eyes opened for a moment, warm and soft and beautiful, before closing again as she whispered his name.

He thrust again, driven by an ancient need. Over and over, until she cried out, begging him not to stop, to never, ever stop.

How he wished it were possible. What a perfect world it would be if they could just stay like that, intertwined in each other's arms, lost in that sensual place where they seemed to be one person.

With each deep stroke, he came closer to claiming her as his—a primitive urge, but he wanted to mark her as his always, so that no matter what happened, no matter when or how they parted, she would always be his.

Deeper and deeper, harder and harder. Her arms closed around him, her fingernails digging into his back as she rose up to meet him, man and woman becoming one.

Pressure built up inside of him. An explosion of need and desire, and when it burst through, he cried out her name, taking her with him as she rose up, her hips meeting his.

He collapsed onto her, slick with sweat, and she stroked his hair.

"What a nice way to wake up," she whispered.

He kissed her cheek, lost in a wave of tenderness he'd never felt for anyone before.

"You make me feel wonderful," she whispered.

"You are wonderful," he said, pulling her close as sleep urged him back into the darkness.

SHE AWOKE ALONE.

From behind a curtain of sleep, she stretched her arm out, seeking his heat, and finding instead only a cold indentation on the sheet.

With a start, she sat bolt upright, lost and disoriented.

"Michael?"

She glanced around the room, listening, but heard no sign of him. Wrapping the sheet around her, she slid out of bed, stepping onto a soggy towel. She stepped over the curious thing, then padded to the door and opened it. She peered outside, hoping to find him walking barefoot on the beach, but already half-expecting that the beach would be silent and empty.

It was. Everything was quiet, her breakfast tray sitting on the table on the porch. She pressed her lips together, tighter and tighter, determined not to cry. Instead, she kicked at the doormat, trying to convert a bone-deep sadness into anger.

No use. And when the mat flew an unsatisfactory few inches, her willpower dissolved and she collapsed onto the porch, pulled her knees up to her chest, and cried.

She wasn't even sure why she was crying, but she couldn't stop. Maybe she was crying about her life back in Texas, maybe for what she'd found on this island, but couldn't hold on to. She didn't know and she didn't care.

All she wanted was to purge herself, to get rid of these feelings, and she let the sobs wrack her body. She didn't even try to hold back, just let the tears come and come until her stomach ached and her eyes burned and she had a nasty case of the hiccups.

They'd shared so much last night, and when she'd fallen asleep in his arms after the second time they made love, she'd foolishly allowed herself to believe that sharing somehow made it real.

But it wasn't real. She'd known that going in, and she needed to keep repeating it. This was a fantasy, and by definition, a fantasy wasn't reality.

It wasn't like she had anything to complain about, anyway. She'd wanted to share a night of passion with Michael, and she'd certainly gotten her money's worth. She was just being silly and stupid if she'd expected that she'd wake up in his arms and they'd spend the day sightseeing together. That wasn't the way the world worked.

She should be ecstatic. Already, one portion of her Fantasies, Inc. request had been fulfilled in spades. She could go back to her marriage to Harold knowing that she hadn't missed out on passion. That she had these memories to sustain her.

Still...just because she could now tick *sexual adventure* off her list, she hoped that didn't mean it was all over. She'd sort of planned on a week of passion-filled nights.

But maybe he didn't feel the same way. After all, he'd left without even saying goodbye.

With a sigh, she stood up and wiped her eyes. Whereas only hours before she'd felt full, now she only felt like a shell of herself.

She wanted to be angry, to cut loose and yell at the top of her lungs, to curse him for leaving her. But she couldn't. She had no one to blame but herself.

She grabbed the coffeepot. Cold. For some stupid reason, that started the tears coming again. She sank to the ground once more, tears streaming down her face as she gazed out over the calm ocean.

Damn. She really wasn't cut out for this fantasy stuff.

7

THE STORM had moved out by dawn, and all the guests seemed to have come out in celebration. By the time Tony had showered and shaved and trekked to the restaurant, all the tables by the pool were full except one. Fortunately, the empty one had an umbrella and a blind side, and he slid into the vacant seat, grateful for the shade and the out-of-the-way location.

Right now, all he wanted to do was sip coffee, let the island's morning sounds drift over him, and think about Kyra. In his own cabana, he'd iced his back again, trying to repair some of the damage he'd done. He'd fallen asleep and dreamt of her. Now he wanted to sit outdoors and think about her some more. He could still smell her on his skin, still feel her kisses on his lips.

He had nothing at all planned for the day, and he intended to use every lazy hour to repeat—over and over until he was certain he wouldn't forget even the slightest sigh, the most delicate moan—every moment spent with her last night. He needed those memories to sustain him for the rest of his vacation. Because no matter how much he wanted to feel the press of her body against his again, he'd come to the unwelcome conclusion that a repeat performance would be a mistake. A huge mistake.

If he'd been thinking clearly, he would have known better than to go to her in the first place. But he'd lost his head, had foolishly assumed that staying anonymous would somehow protect him. Now, though...

If he went back, he was sure to lose his heart. And, frankly, he wasn't sure he could handle that.

She might not know who he was, but he damn sure knew her. Already the thought of walking away at the end of a week made his stomach churn. Better to end it now. A clean break. He'd stay away, she'd never find him, and they'd never have to part. Or, worse, she'd never find out the truth and turn away from him.

It was for the best, and he tossed back a slug of scalding-hot coffee, then closed his eyes and rubbed his temples, determined to focus only on last night...not the lonely nights to come.

"Do you mind sharing?"

Her voice.

When he opened his eyes, there she was, smiling down at him and looking just as beautiful as she had the night before. He tensed, fearing she would recognize him, then exhaled as he remembered he'd shed his disguise. Michael's green eye and beard were gone. And Tony's scar was right there for all the world to see.

He turned in his chair, keeping his good side toward

her. "I'm sorry," he said stupidly, realizing he hadn't processed a word she'd said. "I'm—"

"Tony, right?" She pulled out a chair and sat down. "I'm glad I'm not the only one eating breakfast at noon." She smiled. "I'm Kyra, by the way. We met yesterday."

"Oh. Yeah. Right."

"I'm not intruding, am I?"

"No, not at all. Help yourself."

She filled her cup from the thermos on the table, then unscrewed the lid and looked inside. "Guess I emptied it." She shrugged, then signaled the waiter to bring coffee. "Thanks for letting me join you. There's no empty table and, well, you're the only one I even sort of know."

"I thought you ate in your cabana." The second he said the words, he realized his mistake.

Her brow furrowed. "How on earth would you know that?"

He tried to grin, wasn't quite sure he succeeded. "Stuart," he lied. "He, uh, said all the women ordered breakfast in. And hardly any of the guys did. So, uh, we figured that illustrated some major difference in the sexes, but we didn't exactly know what."

"Oh." She frowned, pondering the conundrum. "Maybe women like to eat in their underwear more than men do."

"Maybe so." He started to reach for her hand, then remembered he wasn't Michael and pulled it back quickly, grappling for something to say to keep her talking, just so he could keep listening to the sound of her voice. "Looks like you went to the trouble of getting dressed. No breakfast in your underwear." Mentally, he rolled his eyes. *Oh, yeah. That's great conversation. Not.*

She glanced down at her outfit, a flowing sundress and a straw hat. "Well, polite society and all that."

"So why did you venture out?"

Her cheeks flushed, and she stirred her coffee absently.

"A wild night?" he asked. He knew he was fishing, but he couldn't help it. If he couldn't spend the day with her as Michael, at least he could spend a few minutes as Tony over a late breakfast.

Her teeth grazed her lower lip, and he could tell she was trying to decide how much to tell him. After a few seconds, she leaned forward, her eyes sparkling. "A spectacular night."

She sat back in her chair and spread the napkin in her lap. "They must have delivered the tray to my door at seven as always. But I didn't even wake up until eleven. When I found the food, it was ice-cold."

"Sounds like you did have a good time last night." He kept his face bland even while his purely male ego was busy congratulating itself. "Someone you met at the party?"

"Not exactly." She waved to a waitress who came over and took her order, then refilled the coffee carafe.

"Did you go? C.J. and I were wondering if you were there."

"You were?" The knowledge that she'd thought about him—about Tony—warmed him. "I...uh... didn't see you."

"Oh. Well, I actually didn't stay very long, so if you came late..." Again, her cheeks turned that adorable shade of pink.

He nodded. "Yeah. I came late."

"I'm sorry I missed you."

"Well, you found me now," he said, as the waitress slipped a huge cinnamon roll in front of her. He caught her gaze and, for a moment, their eyes locked and he thought he saw the tiniest spark of the woman he'd known last night. But she quickly looked down, poking experimentally at her roll with her fork.

"Yes, I did," she said softly. When she looked up, her smile was warm and friendly.

Amazing.

Or maybe not. His friend Alan had no problem with his scars, but Amy did. Kyra wasn't looking at him like a freak, but she hadn't gotten a close look at his face. She also didn't know she'd slept with him, no matter what he might want to imagine.

They were just sitting and talking like friends. And just because Michael had to give her up as a lover, that didn't mean Tony couldn't stick with his original plan and have her as a friend. It wasn't a perfect solution, but at least he'd be around her. Could look at her, talk to her. True, it was a bit duplicitous, but he firmly quashed a twinge of guilt. The alternative was to walk away entirely, and he didn't like that option at all.

"Tony?" Her forehead creased, a little vee appearing above her nose.

"Listen," he said, "I was going to grab a book and spend the day being a beach bum. I don't suppose you'd be interested in joining me."

"An entire day being completely lazy?"

"Yup."

"Sounds like heaven."

He could hear the hesitation in her voice. "But...?"

She lifted one shoulder. "I cleaned out my savings account for this vacation."

"I'm not following."

She didn't answer right away. Instead, she took a bite from her pastry. He knew she was stalling. He could almost see her thinking, trying to decide how much to tell him.

Finally, she put down her fork. "Did you come here for a fantasy?"

"Isn't that against the rules? Asking about other guests' fantasies?"

Her neck flushed, but she held her own, her determined gaze never wavering. "You started it," she said.

"Fair enough." He hadn't planned on the fantasy that had been dropped in his lap, but he certainly couldn't share that with Kyra. "I guess you could say my fantasy was to escape. One of my buddies decided I needed some downtime, and he packed me off here."

"Nice friend. This place isn't cheap. Why'd he think you needed downtime?"

He tensed, then forced himself to relax. Just friends, remember? Summoning all his willpower, he turned his head, then pointed to the scarred flesh that stood out around his left eye.

"Oh." She pressed her lips together. "I'm sorry. That was a stupid question. I didn't mean to bring up—" She shook her head. "Anyway, I'm sorry."

"It's okay. Really." Amazingly enough, right then he didn't give a damn about the scar. He just didn't want her to feel like a heel.

"Well, you may have come to relax, but I came for a fantasy." She grazed her teeth over her lower lip, then looked at him through narrowed eyes. "Promise you won't laugh?"

"I promise."

"I came for an adventure." One shoulder moved in the slightest of shrugs. "There's a little more to it than that, but you get the gist."

He stood up, walked around her chair, then ducked down to see under the table. When he lifted his head, she was looking at him with raised eyebrows.

"What on earth are you doing?"

"Checking out your adventure wear. I'm not sure sandals and a sundress are the recommended attire of thrill seekers."

She laughed, then crumpled her napkin and tossed it at him. "Nut. It just so happens my attire is perfect."

While he gawked like a twelve-year-old, she undid the top five buttons on the dress's bodice, pulled it aside, and revealed a navy blue swimsuit.

"Today's project is scuba diving. And that's why I can't be a bum and lie out with you on the beach."

He sat down again. "That sounds like fun. Where are you going? A reef? A wreck?"

"Not exactly." She pointed behind them to the lagoon-style main pool. "The pool."

"Wow," he deadpanned. "You are a thrill seeker."

She rolled her eyes. "Very funny. Today is the class and tomorrow is the ocean." She propped her elbows on the table and leaned forward. "I've got an idea. Instead of hanging on the beach, why don't you take the class with me?"

THE SECOND the invitation left her mouth, Kyra realized how much she wanted him to agree. She genuinely liked him, and already he'd filled the little well of loneliness she'd been battling since Michael left.

Tony didn't look nearly as enamored with the idea. A riot of expressions were splashed across his face—confusion, disbelief, even a hint of nervousness.

She bit back a delighted laugh, unused to men willing to be even the tiniest bit less than one-hundred-percent macho. "Well?" she prodded.

"Scuba diving," he repeated. "You want me to take scuba lessons with you?"

"It's not like I'm asking you to walk across hot coals," she said, teasing him.

"You might as well be."

With a flash of insight, she realized her mistake. "Oh, I'm sorry. Don't you swim?" She swept a hand around to encompass the island. "Probably stupid, but I just assumed anyone who came to an island for a vacation swam."

He nodded. "I swim. And dive. And horseback ride. And ski."

She imagined that he was extremely good at all those things. The thin T-shirt he wore did nothing to hide the broad expanse of his shoulders and chest, and she'd got a nice glimpse of his well-muscled legs when he'd stood up to tease her about her "adventure wear." He might be spending his vacation lounging in the shade, but she could tell he'd spent his life doing something a heck of a lot more active. No, it wouldn't surprise her at all to find out that Tony Moretti was quite the athlete. But none of that explained why he didn't want to go diving with her. "So you do all that, but you just don't scuba dive?"

"I dive." His face tightened, and Kyra thought he looked almost angry. "At least I used to. But I don't anymore."

"Why not?" She winced. "Sorry. That's really none of my business."

For a moment, his face remained set, distant. She assumed he was silently agreeing, and she mentally kicked herself for being so forward. The man was incredibly easy to talk to, and she'd felt a fast bond, a spark of instantaneous friendship. But that didn't mean he felt it, too. And it certainly didn't give her license to pry.

"Listen," she said, trying to get back onto neutral ground. "I should probably get going. Maybe we can hook up—"

"This," he said, pointing to his eye.

She squinted, trying to follow, but unable to keep up. "Pardon?"

"An accident. I was a firefighter until I got this, and it messed up my back pretty bad, too."

"Thus the need for some R and R." She'd really stepped in it this time. "Look, please forgive me. I spoke without thinking. I didn't mean to open up old wounds."

He reached over the table and took her hand briefly, then pulled away quickly, almost as if he'd been burned. The shock of his fingers against her skin left her hand tingling and the rest of her slightly sad. It was an odd sensation, and not one she was sure she should examine too closely. After all, he was just being polite. Nice men didn't go around touching women they hardly knew.

And nice women didn't feel all tingly from the touch of an island acquaintance.

True enough. Her senses were probably just on hyperdrive. Still, an odd sense of loss washed over her, and she was sorry he hadn't held on. Foolish, but somehow it seemed she knew him better than as a casual acquaintance, and she wished she could offer some real comfort for what was apparently a huge tragedy in his life. Instead, she could only say, "I'm sorry."

He shook his head. "No, I am. I don't mean to dredge up all this stuff. But with the back..." He shrugged, then grinned. "I'd love to join you in P.E., but I've got a note from my mommy."

She laughed. "Are you sure? I always thought water stuff wasn't hard on folks with bad backs. We could ask the teacher."

His gaze drifted toward the far side of the pool where Stuart and a taller man were starting to line up the tanks and other necessary equipment.

"It could be fun," she prodded. "And I'd really love to have you with me."

"I'll watch from here."

She nodded, more disappointed than she should be, but didn't argue. "Maybe we can go hang out on the beach after."

"I'd like that," he said.

They chatted amiably for the next half hour about nothing, and when Stuart waved her over, Kyra realized she wasn't particularly interested in a scuba class—she just wanted to sit with Tony, chatting and laughing. She was perfectly comfortable with him, and the realization that she had a new friend brightened her day considerably.

"Kyra! Come on!"

She waved at Stuart, then smiled apologetically at Tony. "That's my cue."

"So it is."

"You're sure?"

"I'm sure." He smiled, a touch amused, a touch devious. "I think I'll just sit here and watch you fumble about with your gear."

Her eyes widened. *"Fumble?* Okay, fella," she said with a laugh, "now you've thrown down the gauntlet. You're going to see some of the most graceful scuba practice you could possibly imagine."

He sank back in the chair, fading into the shadows as if he were dug in for the afternoon. "I can't wait."

She was wrong, of course. Not only did she soon discover that *graceful* and bulky jackets latched on to heavy air tanks were mutually exclusive—especially out of the water when they were doing the basic skills stuff—but with Tony watching, Kyra felt even more self-conscious.

Every time she looked up, he was smiling at her, the corner of his mouth turned up with just a hint of amusement. He appeared completely relaxed, his large frame filling the lounge chair as he gazed in her direction, as if there was nothing else in the world he could possibly want to do other than watch her learn about buoyancy and controlled ascents.

His attention should have been disconcerting—after all, she hardly knew the man—but instead she found herself flattered, and wishing more and more that he were with her instead of simply watching her.

The instructor, David, stood up and clapped his hands for attention. "Okay, folks, time to buddy up. We're not fully certifying you guys, but we still need to make sure we've got down the basics for an emergency. So we're going to practice buddy breathing. That way if anything happens to your air supply when you're underwater, you can share with your buddy to get back up to the surface."

Kyra had already noticed that most folks were taking the class in pairs—probably couples who'd met through their fantasies. But like her, a few were going it alone. She wondered if one of the single guys was the man Merrilee intended to pair her with if Michael intended on staying away. After all, sharing a mouthpiece underwater, holding tight to each other, and depending on your buddy for pure survival...well, that was both adventurous and intimate.

She sighed, her morning sadness returning for the first time since she'd joined Tony. If Michael wasn't coming back, she wasn't sure she wanted to continue with the sensual aspect of her fantasy. Sun and surf, sure. But sex...

She shook her head. Mona was right. She wasn't the

casual-sex type. She'd fallen hard for Michael, anonymous or not. And if she couldn't have him, she'd just as soon be alone.

On the pool deck, David started matching up all the singles. A nice-looking man with glasses and red hair smiled at her, nodded slightly. She looked away. Probably a perfectly nice guy—and certainly good-looking enough—but she wasn't interested. Not one little bit.

David pointed to a blond guy, about thirty, with a perfectly toned chest and a matching perfect tan. He was moving toward her from the other side of the pool. "Joe," David called, "why don't you be Kyra's buddy?"

Joe's gaze skimmed up her body, and she stifled the urge to reach for a towel to cover herself. "No problem," he said.

No way. She'd much rather hang on the beach with Tony. "That's okay," she said. "I've changed my—"

"I'm the lady's buddy."

She spun around to find Tony standing behind her, gear dangling from one arm, his free hand near his face, clumsily shading his left eye.

Joe crossed his arms over a massive chest. "The divemaster said I was, man."

"The divemaster's wrong."

David looked down and checked his clipboard. "You're not signed up for this class, Moretti."

"I'm not interested in the class. But I'm the lady's

diving buddy. If she's going to practice, she should practice with me."

For half a second, Joe and Tony locked eyes. Kyra tensed, afraid there was going to be a fight, and more than a little baffled that she might be the reason for it. For a moment, the air held a charge, like the calm before a storm. Then Joe backed away, his hands held up in surrender.

"Hey, whatever, man. She's not worth a fight."

"Well, that's why I'm with her," Tony said. "I think she is."

He sat down next to her, his feet dangling in the pool. "I hope you don't mind me muscling my way into your class."

"No," she said, succumbing to a wash of pure happiness. "You can muscle in any time."

THEY DEVELOPED a rhythm—slow, sensual—thirteen feet under the water, with nothing to rely on but each other. Their eyes locked, and the complete trust he saw reflected in her slate-colored eyes warmed his soul. This was the woman he wanted in so many ways. And she wanted him, too.

She just didn't know it.

With a firm grip, he held on to the vest she wore over her swimsuit that held her air tank and her regulator. They were practicing sharing a regulator, and her mouthpiece was dangling free. Her lips were pursed, and she blew a tiny stream of bubbles.

Through the wall of bubbles, she looked at him, her eyes clear through the thin plastic of her mask. Right then, she was totally reliant on him, and he knew with absolute certainty that she trusted him completely.

He inhaled a second breath, then guided the mouthpiece to her. She took it, her hand covering his, and pulled in two breaths of air, her eyes never leaving his.

His free hand held on to her vest, and he could feel her breasts move as she inhaled, the gentle press of her skin against his fingers setting his fingers to itching. He wanted so much for her to know who he was—for her to want him, to want *Tony*, as much as she wanted Michael. But he knew that was impossible.

He'd learned from Amy the hard way that Tony Moretti wasn't lover material, and certainly he hadn't caught any signals from Kyra that she was interested in being more than friends. Hell, he should feel lucky he even had her friendship.

She cocked her head and made an okay sign with her fingers. He nodded, realizing his mind had drifted. *Count your blessings, boy.* Isn't that what the doctor had said?

Well, maybe Dr. Johnston was right. Maybe he should just be satisfied that this wonderful woman considered Tony a friend. Maybe they could even stay in touch once their week was over. A friendly correspondence over the Internet, maybe.

Yes, that was the best solution—cultivate her friendship during the day, and force himself to stay away at night.

She passed the mouthpiece back to him, then gestured to the surface with her thumb.

He nodded, and they linked arms, kicking to the surface together, trading air as they went, their bodies as close as lovers.

It would be hard, getting through the nights without her. But in the end, falling in love with her while she fell for a man who both was and wasn't him...well, that would be even harder.

"YOU STILL haven't told me if I was right," Kyra said. They were baking in the sun, turning golden brown like French fries. Totally unhealthy according to everything she'd read lately, but it seemed almost criminal to go to an island and not go back with a tan.

Tony propped himself up on one elbow, his skin glistening from a layer of sunscreen, the muscles in his arm and shoulder well defined as he turned to face her, sunglasses covering those chestnut eyes she'd learned to read so well while they'd been underwater. She frowned, trying to figure out whom he reminded her of. It was, right on the tip of her—

He pulled the glasses off, and she lost it. *Damn.*

"What?"

"I was trying to figure out who you remind me of," she said. "I almost had it, too."

For a second, he looked almost troubled. "No. I meant what did you mean by 'were you right'?"

"Oh, that." She sat up, swinging her legs over the edge of the lounge chair and digging her toes into the sand. It felt cool, a nice contrast to her overwhelming body heat. She blamed it on the sun, but a tiny, hidden part of her wondered if it didn't have a bit to do with Tony as well. She'd been so thrilled when he'd shown up to be her buddy. And practicing the dive with him, sharing the very air they were breathing, had been so...*intimate.*

And now they were lying side by side on the beach and he was so very, very male. She stifled a shiver. Surely she just had sex on the brain. What other excuse could she possibly have for getting all hot and bothered about sharing a regulator with a friend?

"Are you cold?" He started to roll off his towel.

"No. I'm fine. Just a bit of a breeze."

"Well?"

She frowned. "Well, what?"

He twirled his hand, urging her on. "What was it you were right about?"

"Oh, sorry. My mind's wandering." To forbidden places. This erotic fantasy thing was getting way out of control. "Your back. Wasn't I right that your back did okay in the water?"

He nodded. "Nurse Cartwright, that was a right fine treatment you prescribed."

"Really?"

"Really. A little twinge when we were on the poolside, but when we were underwater, everything was a-okay."

His eyes twinkled, and she couldn't help but wonder if he was talking only about his back.

She pushed away the thought. He'd obviously been through something traumatic recently. The last thing he was probably interested in doing was getting involved with some woman.

This wellspring of passion she'd discovered with Michael was beginning to color her perception of all men, and she needed to rein it in. She and Tony were friends, and that was it. Besides, she didn't want anything more with him. He was decidedly real, not in the least anonymous, and anything more than friendship would be completely out of bounds.

With a flourish, she picked up her daiquiri from the table between them. "To island friendships," she said, holding the glass out.

He grabbed his, and they clinked glasses. "To friendship." He took a sip, then caught her eye. "So, buddy, do you want to grab some dinner with me tonight?"

She thought about it. An evening with Tony, telling jokes, passing the time, enjoying each other's company. A perfect evening, normally.

She slipped her drink back onto the table. "I can't."

"What's wrong?"

"Nothing's wrong." Other than that she was sitting

on the beach with this wonderful man while decadent images of a night filled with Michael filled her head.

"Uh-huh." He raised an eyebrow and looked down pointedly.

She followed his gaze and realized she was twisting her hands in her lap. "Oh."

"Wanna tell me about it?"

She gnawed on her lower lip. Yes, she wanted to tell him, but something was holding her back. Something? No, she knew exactly what it was: guilt. But that was silly. There was nothing but friendship between her and Tony. There couldn't be anything else. So why should she feel guilty for wanting to meet up with her fantasy man? After all, that was the point of Fantasies, Inc., right?

"Kyra?" he prodded. "I take it you don't want to tell me?"

"It's nothing. Really. I just want to get some rest. Call it an early night." She shrugged one shoulder lightly. "I'm not used to spending a full day in the sun, and I'm pretty tired."

"Uh-huh."

"Guess I'm just not a party kinda girl."

"Guess not." From his tone, she was sure he didn't believe her. Even more, she had the feeling he was disappointed in her.

And frankly, she was disappointed in herself. She had nothing to be ashamed of. Besides, Tony deserved better than some casual brush-off.

She took a deep breath. "I lied."

"No kidding."

"There's more to my fantasy than just having an adventure." She licked her lips, trying to find the words. "Or, I guess I should say, I'm not here just for adventures you might find on the ESPN."

"So you're telling me that at least part of your fantasy leans toward The Playboy Channel."

Her cheeks warmed and she realized she'd twisted her hands up in the towel she held on her lap. "I'm not sure about that. But R-rated, at least." She couldn't quite meet his eyes. Somehow talking about...well, *that*...with a man like Tony made her insides flutter even while the rest of her felt foolishly guilty.

"Only *R?*" His voice was light and teasing, and not the least bit judgmental.

"Maybe a touch X-rated." She tried to meet his eyes head on, couldn't, and ended up looking at her hands again. "I mean, I did come here for a fantasy, after all."

"Yes, you did." He moved from his chair to hers and sat next to her. Her breath caught, his nearness disconcerting. But, again, that was just the product of her overactive libido.

"You probably think I'm some sort of loose woman just looking to have a wild time on a tropical island," she said.

"No. I don't think that. But even if that were your fantasy, would that be so bad?" He leaned closer, and she realized she was holding her breath. "I mean, hedonism is a highly underrated hobby," he whispered conspiratorially.

She put her hand over her mouth to stifle a giggle. The man had a marvelous way of relaxing her. "Don't make me laugh. I'm trying to be serious here." She gave him a look of mock firmness, and he saluted briskly as he sat up straight again.

"Roger, that." He took her hand and moved it to his lap. His fingers curled around hers, warm and safe. "Seriously, you want to tell me about it?"

That was the tough question. And what made it even tougher was that she knew the answer so resolutely. "I haven't really told anybody all of it, not even my best friend."

He squeezed her hand, and she wished she could draw on his strength. "No pressure. You just looked like you might want to talk. But if you—"

"No." She turned to look him in the eye. "I mean, yes. I *want* to tell you. I don't know why, but I do."

"Just my boyish charm, I guess." Immediately, he cringed. It was a bad joke, but he'd needed to cover. Just the fact that she felt compelled to share something so personal made him feel special, and he didn't want to do or say the wrong thing.

"I don't know how to say this without sounding sappy," she said, then frowned, her brow furrowing. "The thing is, I don't have that many friends. I guess I'm sort of a loner. My mom died when I was really little, and my family life is pretty intense. My work schedule is even crazier, and that doesn't leave a lot of time for socializing."

"I know what you mean."

"Do you?" She gnawed on her lower lip, then reached up to tentatively trace her fingertip along the edge of his scar. He held his breath, sure she was repulsed. "You said you got this in your job?"

He nodded, but she'd already continued, not waiting for his answer.

"Anyway, what I'm trying to say is that...well...the friends I do have—the *close* friends, I mean, like me and Mona—we just sort of met and hit it off right away. Blam! Instant friendship."

"Like love at first sight."

She blushed, the very tops of her ears turning red. "Well, yeah, I guess you could think of it that way." She turned to face him more directly, tucking her leg under her. "The thing is, I feel that way about you— friendship-wise, I mean," she added hurriedly, even as his insides swelled.

She shrugged, just the tiniest motion of her shoulder. "So, do you think I sound like a sentimental idiot?"

"Not at all." What he thought was that he could fall in love with her, and those were dangerous thoughts, indeed. "I feel the same way." He squeezed her hand, wanting her to realize how much he meant it. "An instant connection."

"It's not at all like me. I'm the most organized person you'll ever meet. Mona calls me anal. I have lists for everything. It's funny that I've made all my closest friends in an instant. Everything else I analyze down to the smallest little detail." She laughed. "It's pretty pathetic, but it's worked for me so far."

"And what is it that you analyze so carefully, Ms. Cartwright?" he asked, leaning back to get a better look at the way the afternoon sun glinted on her sweat-slick skin. His fingers itched to touch her, and he fought the urge. "What do you do when you're not making friends on remote Florida islands?"

"My family owns a chain of radio stations in Texas. We have a syndicated show." She told him a bit about the program and about the day-to-day aspects of her job.

"I know that program. An excellent show."

"Thanks." She looked around, almost distracted, then stood up. "Do you want to walk down to the water?"

"Sure." He got up, resisting the urge to reach for her hand, and followed her to the surf. "Do you still want to tell me about your fantasy?"

"I'm getting there. I guess I just wanted you to realize..." She shrugged. "I mean, I know we hardly know each other, but—"

He put a finger over her lips, silencing her. "I understand." Even more so than he could explain. He didn't get close to people easily. Hell, maybe that's why Amy left. Certainly he'd never felt this connection with her, not like he felt with Kyra. The trick, of course, was figuring out if it was real, or just a product of lust and island magic.

She told him her fantasy, then. About wanting a sensual adventure...and about why: her father, Harold, her decision to marry. At the word *marriage*, he cringed. He'd known all along there was nothing real between them—couldn't be anything between them except friendship. But to know that she was practically engaged...

"What does your dad think?"

She rolled her shoulder with the slightest of movements, as he'd discovered was her habit. "He thinks it's wonderful, of course. He and Harold get along great, he knows we dated for a while when I lived in New York, and his new son-in-law-to-be is going to save the station." She smiled. "What's not to like?"

"Your dad doesn't know, does he?" Tony asked, feeling cold inside.

"Doesn't know what?" The question was spoken innocently, but her face revealed that she knew exactly what he meant.

"That you're marrying this guy out of obligation, not love."

Her eyes flashed. "You don't know that." She looked away, no longer meeting his gaze. "I'd do the same thing whether I loved Harold or not. This is my family. Everything we've ever done is wrapped up in this business."

"Do you really think your father would trade your happiness to save the business? Because you're not going to be happy in a marriage based on a profit-and-loss statement. You deserve more."

A single tear escaped, and she wiped it away with the back of her hand. "I made a promise to my mother," she whispered. "My great-grandfather started this company. It's important to us. It's important to *me*. It's everything I have."

He felt like a heel for pushing her. More than anything, he knew how hard it was to give up a career, how losing it could turn you inside out. Even so, he wanted to grab her by the shoulders and shake her, to convince her she was making a mistake. But he forced his hands to stay by his sides. Not only was that a foolish, knee-jerk reaction, but it would certainly put an end to their burgeoning friendship. She needed a shoulder, someone to talk to, not someone to criticize her decisions—especially not someone who really didn't know about her life.

And certainly not someone who couldn't do a damn thing to help her.

His rescuing days were over, and radio was way the hell and gone out of his league. But he could be a friend to her. No matter how many little deaths he died, he made up his mind he'd be a good friend.

But still some little demon prodded. He needed to know. In his gut, he just needed to know. "You never answered. Do you love him?"

She met his eyes coolly. "I'm going to marry him," she said, killing some tiny bit of hope that he only then realized had been living in him. "He's adored me for years. We started going out because he was interested in my family's business, but it turned into more. He's very good to me, and to my family." She pressed her lips together, and he silently urged her to continue. "But it's not like..."

"Not like?" he urged.

"My fantasy," she whispered, and he knew that she was referring to him—or to Michael, anyway.

"Do you want to tell me?"

"It feels a little weird confessing this stuff to you."

He felt weird, too. Weird and a little guilty. After all, he'd shared her bed, explored her body, watched as she'd opened herself completely for him. But she didn't know, didn't have a clue. His disguise and Stuart's ad-libbed alibi had worked beautifully, and now here he was, pulling one over on this amazing woman.

But what choice did he have? Tell her? If he did that, he'd surely lose her, and that wasn't a risk he was prepared to take. Not talk to her? Also unacceptable. Already she'd worked her way under his skin. He wanted to know everything about her, to be her friend. If he couldn't help her in any real, useful way, at least he could be a shoulder for her to cry on.

What was that saying? The road to hell was paved with good intentions? Well, his intentions were the best, but he was already in his own private hell. And he didn't intend to lose the one bit of heaven he'd run across in a long, long time.

Ignoring his demons, he took her hand and sat down on the sand, tugging her down beside him. The waves rolled in, covering their feet before rolling back out again. "I know it feels weird, but 'instant friends,' remember? You can tell me anything."

She nodded, one quick jerk of the head, and he could practically see her gathering her courage. "He makes me feel so special." She pressed her lips together, blinking, and he was certain she was fighting tears. "It's like he's given me this gift of memories, something I can take back with me."

Damned if she wasn't describing the exact way he felt. His stomach twisted, and he wanted to reach out for her, wanted to wrap his arms around her and hold her tight. Instead, he schooled his face into an expression of polite interest. "Hell of a fantasy man. Did you analyze this fantasy as much as you do the rest of your life? Plotting it out on graphs and charts?"

She licked her lips, looking a little sheepish. "Well...yeah." She sat a little straighter, silently defending her choices. "When I was trying to decide if I should marry Harold, I sat down and made a list of all the pros and cons."

"Since you're gonna marry the guy, I guess the pros won out?"

"Mmm-hmm. I assigned point values, and the pros won by a twenty-two point lead." She shrugged. "So I'm sure I'm doing the right thing, except..." She trailed off, her teeth grazing her lower lip.

"Except some of the cons sounded pretty interesting."

She nodded. "So I made another list. This time of everything I might be missing. And then I applied to come here so I could get everything out of my system in one fell swoop."

"Sounds like a pretty prudent plan."

"Thanks," she said, apparently missing the sarcasm.

She reached out and grabbed his hand, then gave it a little squeeze. "I'm very happy with the daytime adventure part. And I've had at least one good nighttime adventure." She dropped his hand then, shoving her own between her knees almost as if she was embarrassed. "I guess I'll know more about that tonight, huh? I mean, Michael may not come again." Her lips grazed her bottom teeth. "And if he doesn't, I wonder if Merrilee will arrange another encounter." She squinted slightly, as if she'd just tasted something unfamiliar and was trying to decide if she liked it.

"Yeah," he said, suddenly realizing that he'd turned a complete one-eighty. He had planned to stay away, planned to protect his own heart. Now he wondered if Michael was going to have to show up tonight after all. "If he doesn't come...this Michael...if there's someone else..." He took a deep breath. "What are you going to do?"

"I don't know," she said, her eyes sad. "I guess I'll have to wait until tonight's poolside party to see."

He swallowed, unable to stomach the thought of another man touching her. "Yeah," he repeated. "I guess you'll know tonight."

8

LIT WITH tiki torches, Kyra thought the poolside restaurant resembled a fairy garden. Either that, or a nighttime scene from an old episode of *Fantasy Island*. She stifled a giggle. All in all, she'd take Mr. Roarke over fairies any day.

Unless the fairy was the wishing kind. Right now, she had about a dozen wishes zipping through her head, not the least of which was the wish that she knew the identity of her mysterious lover. The problem with anonymous encounters, it seemed, was the difficulty in tracking your date down for a repeat performance.

Of course, she really didn't want to know his identity, had made a studied effort not to try and compare his body to any of the men she saw at the resort. Anonymous was safe. She wasn't sure her heart could stand it if she had to walk away from a man she knew. For half a second, an image of Tony popped into her head, but she pushed it firmly away. She had no business thinking those kinds of thoughts about him. No business at all.

"You look like a woman who needs a drink." C.J.

sidled up and nodded toward the bar. "Can I buy you a beer?"

She pulled herself out of her funk and smiled at him. "I promised myself I was only going to drink exotic-sounding fruity rum drinks."

"We can probably manage that."

She followed him to the bar, set up in a thatched-roof open hut, and watched while he ordered a draft beer and a Razzmatazz.

The bartender dumped some fruit, some ice, and quite a bit of alcohol into the blender, then slid a deep purple concoction in front of her. She eyed it dubiously. "Just what exactly is this?"

C.J. glanced at the bartender. "Kevin?"

"Secret recipe. I could tell you, but then I'd have to kill you."

C.J. shook his head. "That's okay. Merrilee frowns on doing away with the guests." He nodded toward the drink. "Feeling adventurous?"

"Funny you should put it that way." She stuck a tentative finger into the liquid and took a quick taste. So far so good, and so she took a sip through the curlicue straw, pleasantly surprised by the sweet and tangy sensation.

She flashed Kevin a smile. "It's wonderful."

"Well, yeah. I don't go around killing guests for just any secret recipe."

She laughed, warming up to the party atmosphere. "Good plan."

C.J. took her elbow and steered her to a table by the pool. Underwater lights, colored for the occasion, had transformed it into something magical. Not that she really needed the lights. That afternoon she'd found her own bit of magic in the pool. She had so few close friends, and meeting a guy like Tony...well, that counted as something special.

"Penny for your thoughts," C.J. said.

She smiled, sheepish. "Sorry. Wandering mind."

He chuckled. "No, I'm sorry, using an old cliché like that on you. But you look like a woman with a lot to think about."

"I thought I looked like a woman who could use a drink."

"Like I said..."

They laughed, but in the end she nodded. "I was thinking about Tony."

C.J.'s eyes twinkled. "Ah, another island romance brewing? I thought you two kids might hit it off."

"No, no." Her cheeks burned hot. She was uncomfortable thinking about romance and Tony in the same breath. Tony was her friend, hopefully, Michael was her lover. If she could just keep her feelings locked in their appropriate little cubbyholes, she'd do just fine.

Clearing her throat, she looked back up at C.J. "I mean, yes, we hit it off. But it's not a romance at all. We're just friends."

He looked dubious. "I thought you found the boy attractive. What did you say? Something about him being rugged?"

"I said that his scar wasn't that big a deal."

"Is that a yes or a no?"

She blinked. "Yes or no, what?"

"That you think the boy's good-looking." He held his beer bottle up in mock salute. "You need to stick with the program, young lady."

Pushing her hair out of her face—*barrettes*, she needed to remember those stupid barrettes—she leaned over for yet another sip of her Razz-ma-something-or-other. "Now you're just teasing me."

"Pretty and smart. A woman to be reckoned with."

She laughed and took another sip of her drink. If she couldn't be with Tony or Michael, she was delighted to be passing the evening with this man who reminded her so much of her father before his health really started to go downhill.

Fortified by one more pull on the straw, she swallowed and leaned forward. "The truth is, I do think he's awfully good-looking. He's got the most fabulous golden-brown eyes, and this dangerous, roguish quality about him." She frowned. "Except he's not really a rogue at all. I think he just seems that way because he's always wearing sunglasses and sticking to the shadows."

"You've been thinking a lot about him."

"Not that much." In truth, she had. But why not? He

was her new island buddy. "Besides, we're friends. Aren't I allowed to psychoanalyze my friends?"

"Didn't I say you two would get along?"

She nodded, liking the way the word felt in her head. *Friends.* She liked the way Tony filled that role.

"Yeah," she said. "We get along great." She grinned. "Guess you're psychic."

C.J. TOOK the last swallow of his beer, pleased that the two kids had hooked up. "No, if I were psychic, I'd know where your friend was." And he'd know why Tony'd left such a pretty young woman to fend for herself.

"Well, I know where he is." She leaned forward too quickly and almost lost her balance. C.J. put out a steadying hand. "He's hiding in his cabana away from the crowds."

"Leaving you all alone? Not very chivalrous."

"I'm not alone. You're here." One more sip, then she moved closer, urging him to lean in as if for a secret. "And I'm hoping someone else comes along, too."

Someone else? He had a sinking feeling his fledgling matchmaking efforts weren't taking.

"Michael," she whispered.

"The mysterious fellow I've heard about? The one at night?"

Kyra nodded, looking like the cat who'd swallowed the canary. "He's part of my adventure. Or he was." She squinted, then glanced around the pool area. "I was kind of hoping he would be again." She licked her lips. "Actually, I'm a little nervous about it, too."

He looked at her near-empty glass. "No kidding."

Well, he'd tried. Too bad for Tony the pairing of men and women wasn't C.J.'s cup of tea. At least he'd given it a shot.

"Merrilee!" Kyra stood up, a bit wobbly, and waved across the pool deck.

Her call reminded C.J. that he hoped to have better luck matchmaking when he was the man in question. Then Kyra's words stuck home. Merrilee.

Slowly he looked over his shoulder. Sure enough, there she was. Just like always, she took his breath away. She'd been trying to corner him for days now, making appointments that he'd conveniently forgotten, visiting him at the dock so that he had to sneak away just to avoid her.

He really didn't want to avoid her anymore.

No, what he wanted to do was take her in his arms and kiss away the years. But now wasn't the time. Soon he'd tell her everything, and she'd know why her secret admirer seemed to know so many of her secrets.

He hoped she'd be thrilled, ecstatic. Hoped she'd slip into his arms and the years would just disappear.

But he didn't know for sure, and that tiny bit of fear kept holding him back. Soon, though. When the time was right, he'd tell her.

Kyra waved again. "She's not looking this way. I don't think she heard me." She cocked her head, eyeing him. "Too bad, too. She said last night she was looking for you."

"That is too bad." He tugged at the collar of his T-shirt. "You know, I need to run check something in the office." He slid his empty bottle onto the counter. "I'll be right back."

"But Merrilee, she's—"

He patted her on the shoulder and slipped away into the crowd, considering himself lucky he'd managed to avoid her one more time. But it couldn't go on forever. Sooner or later, they'd have to meet. And sooner or later, he'd have to tell her the truth.

He thought of the heart-shaped ruby necklace he'd hidden in his flight bag. Just a few more gifts. A few more, and then he'd fortify his courage and go have a talk with the woman he loved.

Carefully, so as not to attract Merrilee's attention, he slipped behind a stand of potted palms and ran smack into Tony.

"Lord have mercy, you scared the devil out of me."

"Sorry." Tony stepped backward, slipping further into the shadows. "Trying to avoid Merrilee?"

"Eavesdropping's a bad habit, son."

"I've got a lot of bad habits."

The kid tilted his head, one green eye boring into C.J. "Didn't I see you outside of Merrilee's cabin the other night?" He grinned, then leaned back, his arms crossed over his chest. "C.J., old man, have you got a thing going with the boss?"

C.J. took an involuntary step backward. He'd left a wreath of roses along with a bottle of White Shoulders perfume on her bed. The last thing in the world he imagined was that he'd been seen. "Don't be absurd. There's nothing going on. I was just in the area," he lied.

"Uh-huh." Tony didn't look convinced. "What were you telling me about going after Kyra? It was good advice. You sure you're not taking it yourself?"

"I never noticed your eyes are different colors," C.J. said, hoping to change the subject.

The kid shifted, pulling the cap he wore down lower. "Just a trick of the light," he said.

C.J. wasn't convinced. In fact, for the first time, he noticed that, slicked back, Tony's hair seemed darker. And the boy was in desperate need of a shave. Something tickled the back of his memory, and he tried unsuccessfully to grab on to it. "Kyra's over there," he said. "I think she'd love to see you."

"And I think you're changing the subject." The kid leaned against the planter. "You've got a secret, old man. When are you going to tell her?"

C.J. exhaled. He knew when he was beat. "The time's not right. Not yet." He also knew what had been bothering him. The unshaven face. The one green eye. He looked Tony in the eye. "It's hard knowing when to share secrets, don't you think?"

"I've never given it much thought."

"No? Maybe you should."

For a moment, the kid looked startled, but he recovered nicely, and C.J. wondered if Kyra had any clue that her friend and her lover were the same man. Even more, he hoped that finding out wouldn't kill that light he saw in her eyes when she talked about either one of them. Deception was a tricky game.

He knew. He was risking everything for another chance with Merrilee.

But soon...soon he'd share his secret with the woman he loved.

He only hoped that Tony would, too.

SECRETS.

The word hung in the air, raw and accusing.

Tony swallowed and took a step backward. "I don't have any secrets."

"Uh-huh." C.J. nodded toward the bar. "Go see the girl, son."

Tony shook his head, wanting more than anything to go to her, right then. But Tony Moretti wasn't the man she wanted to see. "I'm not the one she wants to see right now. She's interested in someone else." He met C.J.'s eyes. "She's waiting for someone else."

C.J. looked him up and down. "I know. She told me exactly who she's waiting for." He patted the kid on the shoulder as he moved past him. "Good luck, son. Give my regards to Ms. Cartwright."

As C.J. moved past him, Tony wondered if C.J. had figured out his secret identity. The possibility didn't unnerve him too much. After all, the man was part of the staff, so if he did clue in, he'd still be sworn to secrecy. Besides, he knew C.J. liked him; the man wouldn't rat on Tony.

He grinned. C.J. and Merrilee. He had to admit, they'd make a handsome couple. But Tony had never pictured C.J. as the type to sneak around, wooing a woman by playing the secret admirer. There was a history there, and he wondered what the story was. Even more, he hoped C.J. knew what he was doing. He'd hate to see the pilot lose his chance at happiness with the woman he loved.

He pulled the patch out of the back pocket of his jeans and slipped it on. C.J. was right—it was hard to know when to share a secret. Usually. In Tony's case, though, the answer was clear—never.

Kyra had a friend in Tony, a lover in Michael, and a fiancé waiting in Texas. And although he was impressed as hell at her commitment to her dad, he wanted to tell her—beg her—to live her life for herself. Maybe he couldn't be part of that life, but he still wanted her to be happy. And sacrificing herself to a man she didn't really love out of some sense of familial obligation was a recipe for unhappiness.

But he stayed quiet. He was her friend, not her lover. Not really. And if he kept his mouth shut, after this week, maybe they could stay friends. But if he told her the truth, if he risked her marriage and her future simply to satisfy his own ego... Well, what the hell could he do? He couldn't help her. Couldn't save her business, couldn't cure her father, couldn't do any damn thing for anybody.

In the end, he'd lose everything. And even more importantly, he'd destroy her fantasy. And Tony wasn't about to do anything to hurt Kyra. No matter how much doing nothing ripped at his gut.

HE WASN'T COMING. She should pack it in and head back to her cabana. Hanging around the party was foolish. Fantasy or not, Kyra had no intention of hooking up with any man other than Michael. And if Michael had no interest in her...well, she'd packed a few good romance novels. She'd take a long, hot bath and lose herself in someone else's fantasy.

"Buy you a drink?"

She turned, ending up face-to-face with Joe from the scuba class.

"Kyra, right?"

She nodded, her feet itching to move her far, far away, but the rest of her succumbing to good, old-fashioned Southern manners. Damn Texas upbringing.

He glanced at her now empty drink. "Hitting the good stuff early, huh? Kevin makes a great Razz." He lifted two fingers. "Another Razzmatazz for the lady and a shot of tequila with a beer chaser for me."

She cringed, wondering if she'd taken a wrong turn and ended up at a frat party. "No thanks, really. I've had plenty. Just water."

He sidled closer and slid an arm around her shoulder. "Come on, baby. You spent the entire day with that reject from the sci-fi channel. Spend a little time with me."

"Get your hands off me," she said through gritted teeth. She tried to shrug out of his embrace, but he just pulled her closer, leaning down so that she caught the unmistakable stench of far too many tequila shots.

"What's the matter, baby? Don't you want to play doctor?"

"Not with you." She jammed her knee up, catching him where it counts. His arm flew from her shoulder, and his hands flew to his fly, cupping everything he held dear. "Now get the hell away from me."

Bent at the waist and cursing, he still managed to shoot her a withering look. She held his stare until he finally turned and left. "Jerk," she whispered under her breath.

"You're going to put me out of a job."

The low, smooth voice teased her senses, bringing her back to life. She hadn't even realized the sadness she'd felt until his voice washed it away, and she whirled around, sure she was smiling broader than a kid at Christmas.

"How am I supposed to keep up my rep as a chivalrous knight if the damsels rescue themselves?"

"Michael." He was right there, right in front of her. Tall and dark and she wanted nothing more than to throw herself into his arms and erase the memory of

Joe. "I didn't think you were going to come." She pressed her lips together, fighting back a ridiculous flood of tears.

The corner of his mouth twitched up, and he brushed the pad of his thumb under her eye. "I wasn't going to."

Frowning, she wiped her eyes. "I'm not really crying. It's just an optical illusion. Stress. That guy. Hormones." She shrugged. "I don't know. But I'm not really crying. Not really."

Laughing, he slid an arm around her waist. "I didn't think you were."

She leaned in, immediately at home in his arms. She sniffled again. "Why weren't you going to come?"

He kissed her neck, leading her away from the main pool. "A guy could get attached to a woman like you. And getting attached is the last thing a guy like me needs," he said. "But then I asked myself what was worse—leaving you at the end of a fantastic week together, or not seeing you again."

"An attachment is the last thing *either* of us needs," she said, trying to drill the truth into her head. She didn't want or need attachments, strings or emotional involvement. Still, that little voice in her head told her it was too late.

In the end, she'd walk away because she had to—but it was going to hurt like hell.

"TAKE OFF your clothes." He kept his voice low, enticing, and very persuasive.

Her eyes widened, and he fought a smile. "We're in the great outdoors," she said.

"I noticed that." He'd steered them away from the party to the smaller pool area on the far side of the main building. "But there's no one around."

He suppressed a twinge of guilt. She wanted Michael, and she wouldn't want him if she knew the truth. Even if she didn't turn away from his scars, she wanted anonymous. She'd made that very clear their first night.

As Michael, he had the power to make her fantasies come true, and he didn't intend for Krya to miss out on anything. He might not be the most athletic of lovers, but he could be damn creative. If she wanted sexual adventures, then dammit, that's exactly what he'd give her. Wild, wicked, erotic adventures. And he intended to have a damn good time doing it.

"Someone might come."

With a finger hooked under her chin, he tilted her head back, then brushed his lips over hers, supremely satisfied with the way she opened her mouth, inviting his kiss. "That's certainly my plan," he said when they broke the kiss.

Her breath hitched. "No...I...uh, meant someone might see us."

"I know what you meant. But everyone's at the party. And since this pool's locked at ten, no one has a reason to come back here."

She grazed her teeth on her lower lip, and he knew she was intrigued. Good. He wanted her intrigued.

Letting his fingertips graze the top of her ear, he brushed her hair back, then leaned in closer to whisper. "Say yes, sweetheart. Let me make love to you under the stars."

"There are stars over my cabana, too." The words were a protest, but the way her eyes darted to the gleaming pool told a different story.

Slowly, he grazed his hand down her hip, over the sexy little skirt she wore. His fingers touched her skin, and he let his hand roam to the inside of her thigh, the hem of her skirt teasing the back of his hand.

"Nice skirt. Very sexy."

Her breath hitched as she gasped. She tilted her head back, and he trailed kisses down her neck as he slid his hand higher. What he found ripped away his last shred of self-control.

"Oh, man, sweetheart. You're not wearing panties."

She swallowed, and he felt the faint movement in her neck against his lips. "I told you I was hoping you'd come."

"I don't think you have to worry about that." He stroked her center, thrilled by her slick heat. She moaned, crying out his name until he captured her mouth in a kiss. "You realize you've done it now," he whispered when he pulled his lips away. "Now there's no way in hell you're going anywhere else but into that water with me."

Her hands stroked his back. "That far?"

"Temptress."

She kissed the tip of his nose, then twirled out of his arms, her skirt flaring and giving him an enticing view. When he caught her eye, she was smiling, her finger crooked.

"Follow me."

No argument there. He went willingly, a puppy, a slave. The gate was only a few feet tall and easy enough to climb over. On the other side, he eyed the pool, thinking that the cold water was the last thing on earth he needed.

She urged him toward the hot tub, then slipped out of her sandals and stuck her toes in. "It feels wonderful."

"Get in."

Without breaking eye contact, she unzipped her skirt and let it fall to the ground, then peeled off her T-shirt until she was standing naked before him in the moonlight. "Whatever you want." Her smile was seductive and confident, and he wondered just who was seducing whom.

As he watched, she slipped into the water. "What about you?"

"I'm going to find the controls." He found the control box mounted on the side of the changing rooms, and he turned the jets on, smiling at her delighted squeal when the calm water began to bubble around her.

He shed his clothes in a hurry, desperate to feel her against him, then joined her in the water, sitting on the built-in bench as his body adjusted to the temperature change. Without invitation, she came to him, and he found her easy comfort with him thrilling. She planted her knees on either side of his hips, straddling him, and his body immediately reacted.

He fought the urge to bury himself deep inside her, to lose himself in her heat. Instead, he lifted her up, swinging her around until she faced the side of the tub and he was behind her. The water bubbled around her waist, and he drew his hand up her delicate back.

She moaned, and he grazed his hands down to cup her waist.

"Move over here for me." With gentle hands, he moved her in front of the pulsing jet, smiling as she squealed softly when what he had in mind became apparent.

"But I want *you* to touch me."

He slid his hands around, cupping her breasts, as he pressed her back up against him, his hardness nestled against the soft curve of her thigh. "I am touching you." Silently, he slid his hands down to her hips, urging her forward, knowing the jet of water would soon make her crazy.

"Oh, Michael, I—"

"Shhh. Just let go. Let the water touch you. Let me touch you."

With the tip of his finger, he traced a path up her

body, finding her erect nipple and teasing it between his thumb and forefinger. She gasped, then moaned, her hips swaying in a rhythm he'd come to know well.

They stayed like that, the water stroking her, his hands caressing her, as her breath came faster and faster, her excitement pulling him closer and closer. Then finally, she cried out and rocked backward into his arms.

He eased her down onto the bench seat, and she lolled against him, her fingers idly drawing a pattern on his thigh. "Nice," she murmured.

"Sleepy?"

"Mmm-hmmm."

"Maybe I should take you to your cabana and put you to bed."

She turned her face up to look at him, then shook her head just slightly. "Bed? Yes. Sleep? No." She stroked his cheek. "I'm not through with you quite yet."

He chuckled. "Whatever you want. I'm here to make your fantasies come true."

9

AGAIN, morning came without Michael.

This time, she'd known it would. But until she actually woke up alone, she'd been able to hold on to the spurious fantasy that he'd be there next to her. That he'd gather her in his arms and tell her he loved her, that she didn't have to marry Harold and that everything would be okay—her father, her life, everything. That he loved her.

She snorted. Now that really was a fantasy, and not one she needed to be entertaining.

Frustrated, she threw off the sheet and grappled for her robe, then started stalking around the cabana looking for the stupid cell phone. She'd made a big, fat, hairy mistake coming to Fantasies, Inc. Huge. Massive.

How on earth could she go back to a calm, staid life with Harold after sharing such intense intimacy with Michael? After finding Tony, a man she could really talk with? The future loomed before her, and where before it had seemed full of possibility for her career and her family, now it just seemed empty.

Frustrated, she yanked open drawer after drawer, desperately needing a shoulder to cry on.

She found the phone right where she'd left it, of course, and she punched in Mona's number. No answer, not even the machine, which meant either the machine was full or Mona had her computer plugged into the phone line. Either way, Kyra was out of luck.

She considered throwing the cell phone across the room out of spite, but decided that would be even more stupid than falling for her fantasy man. Instead, she put it back in the drawer, took her notebook from the top of her dresser, sat cross-legged on top of the bed, and started tapping her pen against the paper.

The familiar rhythm calmed her, and she tried to focus, remembering why she'd come to Fantasies, Inc. in the first place. A good time. An experience. The experience of a lifetime.

So far, she'd gotten everything she asked for. And despite her whirling, swirling emotions, she'd gotten no more or less than that. There was no *intimacy*. Sex, yes, but nothing more.

She didn't even know him. Just like Mona had said—she couldn't really be intimate with a man she didn't really know, no matter how wonderful he made her feel between dusk and dawn.

This was just a fantasy—a fantasy designed to give her a memory powerful enough to get her through the life that was waiting for her off the island. In the end, she could walk away. She had to.

And in the meantime, she needed to keep the difference between island fantasies and Texas realities firmly in mind.

Determined to pull herself together, she slammed the notebook shut. She considered calling Mona one more time, but ruled it out. After all, there wasn't anything to talk about. She'd have her fling, she'd leave the island, she'd marry Harold. End of story.

Besides, if she wanted to talk there was always Tony. Except...

Frowning, she pulled her knees up and hugged them to her chest. For some reason, the idea of talking about Michael to Tony again just didn't feel right.

She ran a hand through her hair. Yesterday, she'd talked with him about everything. Why on earth would she be feeling shy about running the Michael-problem by him?

Because there is no Michael-problem.

Right. Exactly. That had to be it. She'd already solved the problem, already decided Michael was just her fantasy interlude, so of course she'd feel weird about the prospect of dredging it all out for psycho-analysis by Tony. Besides, there were a heck of a lot more interesting things to talk with him about.

If she was lucky, she could even catch him at breakfast. The thought of spending the day together cheered her, and she hurried to take a quick shower, wondering what kind of adventure they'd share that afternoon.

"HOW ABOUT SAILING?" Kyra asked. Her feet were propped up on an empty chair, a half-empty glass of orange juice in front of her. She took another swig. "It's going to be a gorgeous day. Let's take out one of the boats."

He bit back a frown. His sailing days were over, at least on a small boat where his back would have to take the brunt of the work. "I thought we were diving today."

"We're signed up to go. But we can't talk if we're underwater."

His chest tightened. "What do you want to talk about?" Surely she hadn't discovered his secret, had she?

She shrugged and laughed. "Not a thing. I just like hanging out with you."

He swallowed, the invisible band even tighter now. Trying for casual, he reached across the table and squeezed her hand. "I like hanging out with you, too." Depressing as hell, but he knew the one woman he could talk with, the one woman he could really open up to, could never truly be his. She belonged to another man. Forever, this Harold guy. For now, Michael.

He cleared his throat, knowing he shouldn't bring it up, but morbid curiosity getting the better of him. "So, did your mystery man show last night?" he asked, fighting the urge to tell her everything. He knew he should, that he wasn't playing fair. But he couldn't risk the consequences. She'd be angry, sure, but that he could handle. What he couldn't handle was the pain when she walked away. And that was enough to convince him to keep his mouth shut.

"Kyra," he prodded, "did he come?"

Her cheeks were a delightful shade of pink, and she'd become fascinated with the dew on the outside of her juice glass.

"I'll take that as a yes," he said.

She looked up, her eyes sparkling. "Yeah, he showed."

"And?" God, he was pathetic, but he needed to hear it from her, needed to know.

"And it was wonderful. *He's* wonderful." A shadow crossed her face, and she took another quick sip. "For a temporary fantasy, I mean."

Tony signaled to the waiter, not actually needing anything except an excuse to look away. Damn it all, he was actually jealous. *You're losing it, Moretti.* Kyra had the hots for Michael, and Tony was jealous of his own damned alter ego.

Maybe he should have said yes when the city shrink had suggested he go in for counseling. He sure as hell needed someone to pound some sense into his head.

She cleared her throat. "So how about sailing?"

He shook his head, willing to concede the change in subjects, but not the activity. "Wouldn't you rather relax?"

"What's a little work for adventure-gal?" She cocked

her head, then wrinkled her nose. "Oh, Tony, I'm sorry. I just realized. I bet sailing is hell on your back."

He bristled, then forced himself to relax. "Not at all," he lied.

"Really?"

"Really," he said firmly. "It's all levers and pulleys. Nothing straining at all." Another lie.

"Sounds like work. Kevin said the big boat's going out this afternoon," she said. "All we'd have to do is hang out on the deck and drink daiquiris."

"That doesn't sound very adventurous."

"Well, no..."

"Let's go sailing," he said. "The back's not a problem." His nose was going to start growing if he kept this up, but he didn't want to see pity in her eyes. Not from her, never from her. "I promise."

The truth of it was, he wanted her time on the island to be special. Maybe he couldn't confess, but he could damn well try to make her fantasy perfect—her days with him, and even her nights with his damned alter ego. Sensual, erotic, unforgettable.

"You really want to go?" She still didn't sound convinced. Smart girl, but he couldn't stomach her thinking him helpless. And so long as the weather cooperated and his back held up, he wouldn't be. Besides, she wanted this, and in some small way taking her out on a boat might assuage some of the guilt sitting like a lump in his stomach.

"Absolutely," he said. "We'll go tomorrow."

She smiled, and he knew he'd finally convinced her. "Sounds great, so long as you're sure."

"Absolutely. We'll have a blast." He kept his face calm, hoping against hope the Fates—and his lower lumbar region—were on his side. "I can't wait."

"TELL ME about your day," Michael said, his voice softer than the candlelight glowing in the small bathroom.

Sighing, she leaned against the side of the deep tub, sliding down until the bubbles grazed her breasts. Michael balanced on the edge behind her, dribbling warm, soapy water from a sea sponge onto her bare shoulders. Pure heaven.

"It was wonderful," she murmured, her voice near a purr. And it had been. Tony knew his way around the island better than she knew a radio control booth. He'd shown her all sorts of secret places, and even rescued a baby bird from a tangle of fishing line. They'd forged onward through the humid air, battling the foliage. Even now, she could picture the nape of his neck, the way his sweat-dampened hair curled above the collar of his T-shirt. And the way he'd kept glancing back at her, so protective, had practically given her chills.

They'd finally ended up at a crystal-clear pond, deep in the wilds on the north side of the island, and they'd spent the day skipping rocks and talking about everything and nothing. She'd told him about wanting to make the station a success, wanting to make her father proud. He'd told her about his former life as a fire-fighter, all the lives he'd helped save, and sharing his dream that he'd someday be able to do something else to help protect people.

"A great day," she repeated.

"I'm glad to hear it." He slipped his hands down into the water, stroking her breasts until she closed her eyes and arched up, her body silently demanding more. "Let's see if we can't make the night just as great."

"Shouldn't you be out saving kittens or something? It seems like you're always with me." She opened her eyes and grinned. "Not that I'm complaining."

"I'm exactly where I want to be," he said.

"Good." She tilted her head back and sighed, her body thrumming from the touch of his strong hands on her breasts, her stomach. "Because you're exactly where I want you to be, too."

THE BOAT moved along at quite a clip, the sails billowing in the strong wind. Kyra stood at the front, her arms out to her sides, *Titanic*-style, as they flew over the vivid blue sea.

Her hair whipped around her face in a mass of tangles. Her nose shone with a coat of yellow zinc oxide. Her T-shirt was stuck to her skin from the ocean spray. She felt wonderful, almost giddy, and she turned around to smile at Tony. "This is fabulous!"

He looked up from the back of the boat where he

was busy doing something, then cupped his hand to his ear.

"Fabulous!" she repeated, and he nodded.

"Wait a sec," he called. She stayed put, stifling the urge to touch anything until he told her to, and fearful that if she moved toward him she'd get whonked in the head with some moving part. She watched him work, enjoying the way he moved and the way the sun glinted off the purely masculine angles of his body. After a few moments, the boat slowed to a stop, the sails hanging slack, and she realized he'd dropped the anchor. She'd been so caught up watching him, she hadn't been paying attention to what he was actually doing.

"This seems like a good place for our picnic," he said.

She blinked, dragging her mind back to reality as she took a look around. In the distance, she could make out the shoreline of Intimate Fantasy. To her left—*port,* he'd said—waves were frothing, breaking on a reef that rose up to skim the surface of the tantalizingly clear water. Clouds moved in the sky, billowy mountains of cotton playing peek-a-boo with the sun. "It's perfect. I'll get the basket."

The restaurant had packed them a lunch, and she made her way down below to the tiny cabin under the deck. The place was adorable—a little apartment in miniature, complete with a tiny portal window. She cranked it open, letting in the breeze, then grabbed the basket and went back up top.

He'd spread a blanket on the deck, and now he was stretched out, his sunglasses tossed aside as he lay back basking in the sun. For a moment, she just stood there, mesmerized by the way the sweat glistened on his bare chest. Already, from just their few days together, he'd gone from slightly pale to a rich bronze. Her throat hitched, and she tamped down a wash of sadness for this wonderful man who'd been hiding himself from the world inside because of one stupid accident that had left him scarred, inside and out.

Thankfully, he was becoming less and less self-conscious. She glanced at his sunglasses, thrilled he'd taken them off with absolutely no chance of shade. He trusted her, knew she couldn't care less about the angry scar that rimmed his eye. Knowing he felt that comfortable with her made her feel warm and special.

Ironic, really. A week ago, she'd been alone. At least, it had seemed that way. And now she had two men in her life who made her feel like the center of the universe.

She tamped down a twinge of guilt. She was never the kind of girl who could date two men at once, could never understand how those girls in high school did it. Kyra had always become too involved, unwilling or unable to spread herself too thin. But now she was spreading herself between Michael and Tony, and the situation made her feel strange and awkward.

That was silly, of course. No matter how special Michael might be, he was still a fantasy, still anonymous. And no matter how dear Tony was, there was nothing physical between them. They were just friends, that's all they'd ever be. The thought made her a little sad, and she frowned, trying to shove away her melancholy mood.

She plopped down next to him and started unpacking the basket. When everything was spread out, she gave his foot a gentle nudge. "Hey, sleepyhead. You hungry?"

He rolled over, mumbling something, and she was struck with an odd sense of déjà vu—like she'd woken up next to him before. She shook her head. Silly. He just had the same build as Michael, and they'd spent so much time together that now everything about him seemed familiar.

Another kick, this one a tad more forceful. "I'm going to eat everything and there won't be anything left for you."

He sat up blinking, looking adorably like a sleepy little boy. "Even my brownies?"

"Well..." She grabbed the brownies in question, holding on to the foil package.

He scooted closer. "It's dangerous to keep a man from dessert," he whispered, his voice low, menacing and oddly familiar.

"Whatever do you mean?" she asked, all innocence as she clutched the brownies closer.

"Careful, little lady." He grabbed her around the waist, tickling, and she gasped, the feel of his arms around her both playful and exciting. "Come on, sweetheart. You know you can't win."

With a massive effort, she focused on their game, not the riot of sensations rippling through her. "Help!" she squealed, "I'm being attacked for my dessert!" She rolled backward, pulling him down with her while still holding the brownies against her chest. He was just inches away, so close she could feel the press of his body against hers and the warmth of his skin. Her breath came in jagged bursts and she tried to get a handle on her confused emotions.

"Got you," he said. His hands brushed her breasts as he reached for the brownies. His face was only inches from hers, his touch and scent both welcome and familiar. They were both breathing hard. For a moment, everything else disappeared. The sound of the waves, the whisper of the wind against the sails, the call of birds overhead. All gone. Just her and him, alone.

Her lips parted in some unconscious invitation, but then she caught herself and snapped her mouth shut, blinking and shivering. Suddenly antsy, she shifted beneath him, unsure and needing to get away. Maybe he felt it, too, because he pulled himself up, flashed her a weak smile, and took the package of brownies to the far side of the blanket.

"Want one?" he asked, so calmly it irritated her.

Didn't he feel it? Or was her overwrought libido playing tricks again? "They're good," he added.

She shook her head, not trusting herself to speak. "No thanks. I'm fine." She wasn't fine. She was a long way from fine, but she didn't intend to share that little fact.

After a minute, she grabbed a bottle of water out of the ice chest and took it to the front of the boat, letting the strong wind whip around her, beating away her frustrations. She glanced back over her shoulder, but he hadn't followed. Instead, he had his face tilted up to the sky, his eyes closed, looking perfectly at peace with the world.

She turned back to the sea, now restless. Just looking at him had warmed her to her toes, and the knowledge made her uneasy.

The waves were breaking harder over the reef, and the reef seemed even closer now. She squinted. It *was* closer. That was odd. And the sun no longer kissed the deck's polished wood.

The clouds that had followed them had suddenly turned nasty, were now black and ominous. Something clanked against the boat's hull, a metallic warning for them to get out of there. Like summers in Texas, storms over Florida developed fast, and this one looked to be a doozy. She twirled around, about to call for Tony when she realized the boat was moving, drifting backward closer and closer to the reef.

That couldn't be good.

"Tony!"

He was already looking up, frowning as he stared at the clouds. He turned toward her voice, and she pointed.

"We're moving," she said.

The wind raced over the boat, slapping her hair into her eyes and sending it stinging against her skin.

"It's okay. We're anchored. You're just feeling the boat rock. We'll be fine until the squall blows by, but we should go below. I don't think it'll last too long."

"No," she shouted over the wind. "It's really moving." She looked out toward the reef again. "Take a look."

He did. "Damn. You're right. We're dragging anchor."

The boat rocked upward as the waves got into the groove of the storm, and she grabbed on to the side as the front end slapped back down against the water, sending ocean spray shooting up into the air.

Tony stumbled toward her, trying to keep his balance on the rocking boat. The front dipped down as yet another wave crashed over the boat, and she was thrown forward. He caught her around the waist.

"I need to get the anchor up."

She moved toward the front, where the rope hung down, taut now from the pull of the current. "I'll help."

He shook his head. "I need you in the cockpit."

She didn't argue, but he must have seen her confusion. "I need you to nudge the engine forward. That'll give me some slack so I can pull up the anchor." The boat tossed once again, and he grabbed her shoulders, bracing them both against the stomach-churning motion. "Do you remember how?"

She nodded, wiping the spray off her face, then turned and carefully picked her way to the cockpit. When she turned back around, she saw Tony sprawled out over the front of the boat tugging at the anchor line, but the drag of the boat still pulled it too taut, and he wasn't having any success at all.

The boat heaved, a huge wave crashing up as the nose went down. Kyra screamed as a wall of water broke over Tony. She held her hand to her mouth, chewing on her knuckles, until he turned around and signaled that he was okay.

He yelled something that she couldn't hear, but she gave him a thumbs-up anyway, certain he wanted her to ease the boat forward and give him some slack. With her hair flying, she concentrated on the controls, trying to remember the crash course he'd given her when they'd set out that morning. After a hesitant start, she got the engine to cooperate. Forward, then halt. He'd take up some slack. Then forward, and halt again. And over and over, until they'd found a rhythm working together, not needing words, but somehow communicating as they worked together to get the best of the storm.

Tony secured the anchor, then clambered over the deck to her. "Great job." He adjusted the boat, then put her hands back on the wheel. "Just hold us steady for a bit."

After fiddling with the sails for a few moments, he came back and took control. "You okay?"

She nodded. Already the storm was dying. But still her pulse throbbed so rapidly she could barely tell where one beat stopped and the next began. She was soaked to the skin. She still couldn't catch her breath.

All in all, she was more than okay. She felt wonderful.

"When you promise a girl an adventure, you deliver." Impulsively, she raised up on her toes, wanting to kiss him, to hold him close. Wanting to continue that awesome feeling of togetherness, like they were joined in mind and body, moving in a timeless rhythm.

But as she moved in closer, she saw the surprise and shock reflected in his eyes, and managed to catch herself just in time. Embarrassed, she took a step backward, twisting her hands in front of her.

"Kyra?"

Mortified, she couldn't meet his eyes. "I...I left the portal open down below. I better go make sure we haven't flooded the cabin."

Careful not to stumble in the drizzle, she hurried below, then threw herself onto the bed. She grabbed a corner of the spread and wiped her face, not sure if she was drying rain or tears.

She needed to get a grip, needed to get her emotions under control. This was just hormonal. PMS, probably.

Sure. That's all. Just an emotional reaction to riding out the storm together.

Nothing had changed. Nothing important, anyway. In just a few days she'd go back to Texas and tell Harold she'd marry him. She'd get her life under control, take care of her business and her father. She had a plan, dammit. A good plan. A solid plan.

She was already confused as hell about her feelings for her anonymous Michael. The last thing in the world she needed was to fall in love with Tony Moretti.

TONY MOVED on autopilot, his concentration intense as he ignored the pain and focused simply on getting them back to the island. Only when he'd reached the dock and secured the mooring lines off did he let the full impact of what he'd done register. *Idiot! Damn him to hell, he'd been an arrogant, pathetic son of a bitch.*

He should have known better than to take the boat out with his back—he *did* know better. But he'd ignored his common sense and they'd almost been dragged onto the reef.

He'd wrenched the hell out of his back trying to pull up the anchor. If he hadn't been able to fight his way past the red surge of pain...if Kyra hadn't been cool enough to remember how to maneuver the engine to give him some slack...

But dammit, he shouldn't have put her in danger in the first place. Shouldn't have lied about his abilities just to impress her. He should have told her the truth and let someone else take her sailing.

What if the storm had been worse? What if—

Bile rose in his throat, and he lurched forward, almost losing the contents of his stomach.

He could have killed them—could have killed her. And all because he wanted to prove that he was as whole as any other man. That he was as whole as she thought Michael was.

But he wasn't whole, and he never would be.

He clenched his fists, furious at life, at his predicament, at everything—but mostly furious at himself for putting her at risk, this woman that he'd come to care for more than anything or anyone he'd known before.

And he remembered how she'd backed away, her eyes wide and mortified, instead of kissing him.

"Tony?" she said. "Are you okay?"

He looked at her, saw the worry reflected in her soft gray eyes.

No, he wasn't okay. He hadn't been okay for almost a year. And it was about damn time he came to grips with that. About damn time he accepted his fate and got on with his life.

10

LOVE.

Alone in her cabana, the word taunted her, keeping her from sleep. Could she really be in love with Tony? Her head screamed no, but her heart whispered yes.

The rest of her was just confused.

Sighing, she flopped back on the bed and pulled the pillow over her head.

She was having the time of her life, but with two different men, and it was making her a little nuts. What she wished more than anything was that the man she loved during the day was the same man who she made love with at night.

That word! There it was again. No matter how much she wanted to hide from the truth it kept finding her— she loved Tony.

The knowledge made her giddy, and she actually giggled. She'd never been in love before, not really, and it felt wonderful. Even if it couldn't last, even if it was only fleeting, when she was old and feeble she could look back on her life and remember that she'd been in love. Really and truly in love.

She loved the way he laughed. The way he'd made

her feel comfortable. The way they seemed to fit together, to feed off each other's thoughts. The rhythm on the boat, the buddy breathing—heck, just hanging out on the beach.

She hugged the pillow tighter. She'd been so worried about avoiding strings with Michael that she'd forgotten to worry about the kind of tie that was stronger than sex. Intimacy. And the only man who'd really gotten that close to her was Tony.

Michael was sweet and wonderful and she'd shared some amazing things with him, but in the final analysis, their relationship was lacking. But with Tony...well, that went a lot deeper. He grounded her, made her feel safe and special. Oh Lord, she loved him. So help her, she did.

And that created a little bit of a problem. She certainly couldn't keep sleeping with Michael now that she realized she was in love with Tony.

She sat bolt upright as an even more disturbing problem occurred to her: How on earth could she marry one man if she was in love with another?

A tricky question, true, but she had the answer. The same answer she'd had all her life—family obligations, responsibilities, plans.

She blinked back tears. She'd marry Harold because she had to. She'd hold on to Tony's memory because she wanted to.

Isn't that why she came to Fantasies, Inc. in the first place?

Outside her window, the sun dipped below the horizon, painting the sky in a fabulous array of oranges and purples. She watched the spectacle until one sharp knock at the door interrupted.

She pulled open the door, then fought back a gasp. *Michael.* An unexpected wave of disappointment flowed through her. She'd had no reason to expect Tony, none at all, and yet somehow that had gotten in her head. Certainly he'd gotten in her blood, and the thought of being with Michael now simply depressed her—no matter how much the touch of his hands made her body sing. She felt her eyes well up.

In one fluid movement, he kicked the door shut and gathered her in his arms. "Hey, baby, shhhh. What's the matter?"

Feeling foolish and silly but unable to stop, she let the tears come. She kept her face pressed against his shoulder, breathing in the now-familiar smell of his cologne. He stroked her hair and she relaxed in his embrace, letting herself take some comfort from him as she gathered her courage.

His hands closed on her shoulders and he gently pushed her away. His face was firm, studying hers. "Kyra? What's wrong?"

Everything. Everything and nothing.

"I...I don't think we can do this anymore."

His grin was lighthearted, but she could see the undercurrent of concern. "This?"

She stepped back, breaking the contact between

them, and swept her arm out to encompass the room. "Yes. *This.* All of this. You and me. I can't do it anymore." A tear trickled down her face, and she wiped it away.

"Sweetheart, I—"

She put a finger over his lips. "No. Please. I'm sorry. You do things to me. Truly amazing things." She closed her eyes, gathering her courage even as she remembered how wonderful he made her feel. "But I can't do it anymore." She looked him straight in the eye. "I'm sorry."

"Why?"

She took a deep breath. "I realized that I'm in love." It felt good to say it, as if saying the words aloud made her stronger. As if Tony was right there beside her spoon-feeding her courage.

Michael stiffened. "Who's the lucky guy?"

He sounded almost anxious, and a tingle whispered up her spine—another curious déjà vu, and again she pushed the sensation away, attributing it to her own fragile emotions.

She opened her mouth, wanting more than anything to say that she was in love with Tony. Wanting to say his name out loud and make it truly real, make it final.

But she couldn't.

She couldn't give up the life Harold had offered her, couldn't sacrifice everything her family had worked so hard for, couldn't turn her back on her promises to her mother.

"Kyra," he repeated, his voice firm. "Tell me who you're in love with."

She looked up, meeting his eyes. "I've got a fiancé back home. I'm going to marry him."

"You're in love with him?" Disbelief laced his voice.

She pressed her lips together, unsure how to answer. But then she looked up into his eyes and knew he deserved the truth. "No. But I like him. I trust him, and I respect him." She tried to smile. "I'm sorry, Michael. I just can't do this anymore."

"But if you don't love him? If you love someone else..."

A single tear rolled down her cheek, and she wiped it away. True, their relationship had been mostly physical, but they'd shared so much. She owed the man an explanation at least. She'd told Tony about her fantasy. At the very least, she should tell Michael as well.

"I never really told you about my fantasy," she said, "about why I'm here, about why I wanted you to be anonymous." She stroked his roughened cheek, running her thumb along the bottom of his eye patch. "I've got obligations. Family stuff. Promises I made. I *need* Harold." She shrugged, accepting her fate, knowing what she was giving up, but certain she was doing the right thing. "I need him, and I'm going to marry him."

SHE STOOD in front of him, her back straight, perfectly calm. But she might as well have just kicked him in the gut, just reached in and ripped his heart out.

Certainly, he couldn't feel any worse.

She loved him. Tony. Him. He was certain of it. His amazing Kyra had looked past the scars and seen *him*. And she loved him.

But that didn't matter. Kyra loved Tony, but Harold had won anyway. Good old Harry got the girl, was going to spend the rest of his life with the woman Tony loved.

He started to open his mouth, wanting to argue with her, to beg, to plead. Wanting more than anything to tell her he loved her and to urge her to stay with him forever.

But he said none of it. Tony didn't have the right stuff, and Harry did. Good old Harry could rescue the girl, could secure the castle and keep out the barbarians. Tony didn't have a damn thing to offer. Nothing except love, but why even open that door? In the end, it would only hurt more, because Kyra had already made it clear that love wasn't calling the shots where her life was concerned. It would hurt him, and it would hurt her.

Better to keep their friendship alive, even if that meant he died a tiny death. Better to see her, to laugh with her, to spend time with her. She'd need a friend, after all. And in the end, that was the most he could do. Be a damn good friend to her. Or Tony could. Michael needed to just leave her alone.

He reached out for her and, after a moment of hesitation, she slipped into his open arms. He held her close, then kissed the top of her head. After a moment, he pulled back and looked at her red and puffy eyes.

"I'm going to go now."

She nodded, and he slipped out of the cabana, shutting the door behind him. He walked along the beach to his own room, stopping only once to hurl a rock into the churning waves.

Numb. He felt numb. He'd lost her today. Ever since the accident, he'd expected to lose any woman he got close to. But this had blindsided him. He hadn't lost Kyra because of his face or his back or anything. All those problems, all those hours of self-pity, and at the end of the day, his physical appearance wasn't the problem. He should have known Kyra wouldn't care about that.

Trouble was, what she did care about was way out of his league.

As he opened the door to his cabana, the theme song from *The Lone Ranger* rang out. His cell phone. It had to be Alan, and he snatched it up.

"Moretti."

"Yo, Tony. You keeping the babes satisfied?"

"All the time," he said.

"You okay?" Alan's voice turned serious.

"Fine," he said. Then, "No. I'm not okay. I'm not okay at all."

To his credit, Alan kept the sarcastic comments to a minimum, actually listening as Tony told him everything.

"Your back must be getting better," Alan said. He had yet to comment on Kyra, and Tony had to smile. Leave it to Alan to tackle the easy problems first. "I mean, if you're running around being this Zorro character—"

"So what? I'm supposed to head back home and tell the chief 'Hey, put me back on payroll. I saved a kitten from a tree'?"

"You told me the kitten got away."

"Very funny." But Alan was right. He'd been coping with his back these past days. It wasn't great, but he'd been coping, ignoring the pain to play the hero, to live out his fantasy.

"You know what I'm saying," Alan said. "So you're not back on active? Big deal. You can work a desk. Or get another job. That consulting firm. Hell, they're nationwide. You could live anywhere in the country—even Texas," he added in a very Alan-esque way of steering the conversation around to Tony's real problem.

Tony ran his hands through his hair. Maybe there *were* other ways to be useful. Maybe he didn't have to be out fighting fires. Maybe he could even get some satisfaction behind a desk.

But that didn't change the most basic fact. "I can't help her, Alan. She needs a deep pocket. A businessman. Someone with more money than I've ever seen. Someone who can keep a family legacy alive." Frustrated, he clenched his fist. "This is the woman I love, and there's not one damn thing I can do to help her."

Even as he said it, he had to wonder. Why hadn't he told her he loved her? Were his reasons really that noble, or was he just afraid of the pain he'd feel when she aimed those sad eyes at him and still chose Harold?

It was a risk. She might turn him down, might hang tooth and nail on to that foolhardy plan of hers. But dammit, he had to try.

He drew in a deep breath and said goodbye to Alan.

It was time for Michael and Tony to go have a talk with the woman they loved.

SHE WOKE UP confused and not rested at all. Weird thoughts and images had danced in her dreams, and she'd spent the night tossing and turning. She wanted to call Mona, but her friend would just say that her insomnia was the product of typical Kyra-guilt—she loved one man, was sleeping with another, and yet planned on marrying another one altogether.

But that wasn't it, not exactly. Stretching, she grabbed her notebook from the bedside table and trained her eye down the list she'd made before trying to sleep. Every reason why she should marry Harold was neatly printed down the left side of the page—her family, the business, security, stability, and more. All there in black and white.

On the right side, she could only put one reason not to marry Harold—Tony.

No contest. The pros clearly won out, though she was having a few niggling hesitations about following her list rather than her heart.

Still, something else was bugging her—that déjà vu feeling she'd been having for the past couple of days.

Annoyed, she rolled over, burying her head under the pillow. She'd left the Do Not Disturb sign up, and the maid hadn't changed the sheets. Now she breathed in Michael's familiar scent.

Very familiar.

She sat up, confused, as an image danced on the edge of her memory. The boat. When she'd play-wrestled Tony for the brownies. That scent. She knew it, was smelling it right now on her sheets: Obsession.

Coincidence, or more?

"Now you're being silly," she whispered. Her imagination was clearly running wild.

Or maybe not so wild. She nibbled on the edge of her thumb as her mind sifted through clues. The patch over his left eye and Tony's scar. The evening beard and Tony's freshly shaved face. Michael's insistence on the dark.

But that was silly. Tony had been off the island the night she met Michael, or at least that's what he and Stuart had said. A constructed alibi?

Maybe.

Except Tony had a bad back, and she and Michael hadn't exactly been calm in the lovemaking department. But even then...

She frowned. Even then, Michael had been careful. The first time they'd made love, she'd been on top. And the other times...she sighed, her body remembering his touch. Yes, he had been careful.

She recalled the soggy dishtowel she'd found on the floor by her bed. Melted ice, perhaps? Maybe even being careful, his back had paid the price.

Her breath caught in her throat, and she sat up straighter. It was true—it had to be. The man she loved and the man she made love with were one and the same.

Michael was Tony's secret identity. And Tony Moretti was her fantasy lover.

A wave of pure happiness washed over her, only to be replaced by a flash of anger.

He'd lied to her. Both of them—Tony and Michael. He, they, *whoever*, had lied to her.

Every day, she'd left Tony for her secret lover, while all the time he'd known exactly who she was running to. And with Michael she'd tried so hard to keep their relationship purely physical. No strings, no nothing. Yet all the time he knew her little secrets, every detail she'd shared with Tony during the daylight.

She tried to hold on to the anger, wanted to nurture it and keep the sadness in check. But it was useless; she couldn't stay mad.

She knew Tony. Knew him well enough to fall desperately in love. And that meant she knew him well enough to know the depths of his insecurities.

He hadn't told her who he was for fear she'd turn away. He'd protected his heart, and in doing so, he'd protected her fantasy. Hadn't she told him a million times how important anonymity was to her?

Well, she'd gotten anonymous all right. But she'd never expected her fantasy to turn around and bite her on the butt.

Be careful what you wish for...

She pulled her knees up, hugging them to her chest, and when the tears came, she didn't even try to fight them.

So much had changed in the past twenty-four hours. *She'd* changed. And even though she'd fought her feelings tooth and nail earlier, deep in her heart, she knew she couldn't go back to Texas and marry Harold.

She had no idea how she'd save the business—or even if she'd be able to save it—but Tony was right. She did deserve more than a marriage based on a profit-and-loss statement. Harold deserved a woman who truly loved him. She deserved a man whom she loved, and who loved her right back. Just like her mom had found in her dad.

It was scary, risking the business when she could so easily save it. Just two little words—I do. But those were two words she couldn't say without three other little words, not even for her father. A week ago, yes. But things had changed. She'd changed.

She'd fallen in love, and she owed Tony the world for opening her eyes.

She needed to tell him, and the thought made her smile...until she remembered—*she'd already told him.*

She'd stood right there with Michael and said the magic word—*love.* Had said she loved him. Certainly it had been clear enough. He knew she didn't love Harold, and that left only Tony.

She'd taken the risk, said it out loud and still he hadn't dropped the facade. Hadn't said the words back to her. Hadn't argued when she'd said she was going to marry Harold. Hadn't tried to talk her out of it. Hadn't even blinked.

She sniffled, determined not to cry. Love wasn't always a two-way street. If he didn't love her, she'd still survive. After a while the pain would lessen and she'd have her memories. Heck, that was more than some people had in a lifetime. She should be grateful, but she wasn't. Instead, she felt like crawling back under the covers and crying buckets.

She was just about to do that when the door opened. Squinting, she leaned forward, just in time to see black jeans, a T-shirt, dark hair and an eye patch.

Her breath caught. Michael. Tony. Either way, the man she loved.

And, dammit, she wasn't ready to give up yet. Maybe he hadn't said the words, but did that really mean he didn't feel them?

She didn't know. Not for certain. But she damn sure intended to find out.

"I NEEDED to see you," he said, hoping she wouldn't send him away. "I want to talk to you." He needed to confess all. And he needed to tell her he loved her.

"I'm glad you came." She was in her bed, the sheet covering her legs. He saw her shorts on the floor and imagined she had very little on under the covers. He swallowed and reminded himself to keep his eye on the ball, not her skin.

"Why's that?"

She patted the bed next to her, her grin slightly devious. "Maybe I decided I wanted another night with you, another erotic encounter."

She let the sheet slip back, revealing her thin T-shirt and a good deal of bare leg. He swallowed. They needed to talk, needed to settle this, but the lure of having her in his arms again enticed him beyond belief. A man was only so strong....

He fought the tug of attraction. Not until she knew the truth. He wasn't going to lie to her again by omission. He wasn't going to make love to her again under false pretenses.

"What's the matter, Michael?" She knelt on the bed, then moved toward him. When she was just a few inches away, she reached out and caressed his cheek. "I thought you might like to know that I've decided to call off my marriage."

He swallowed. So much for rescuing. Once again the damsel had saved herself. "You have?"

"Uh-huh." Her fingers teased the corner of his

mouth, and without thinking he parted his lips, welcoming the taste of her. "Do you want to know why?"

Barely able to form coherent thoughts, he simply nodded.

"I thought about what you said."

"About not loving your fiancé?"

"About deserving more. About not being happy in a marriage based on a profit-and-loss statement." She met his eyes. "You were right."

"I was?" His breath hitched as he realized the import of what she was saying. He'd said that on the beach, days ago. *As Tony.* "No, I never said that," he whispered.

She met his eyes, her nod almost imperceptible, as she reached up to stroke his face. Her fingers deftly skimmed under his patch, pushing it up and off before he could stop her. "Yes, *you* did."

He stiffened, afraid she'd be angry. But when he looked in her eyes, he saw only understanding. "I'm sorry," he said. "I should have told you earlier."

"It's okay. I understand why you didn't." She looked down, and he noticed that she was twisting her hands in her lap. "But there is one thing I'm not as sure of—"

"I love you." He took her hand. "I love you, Kyra."

Her smile was watery, and she closed her eyes, her relief almost palpable, and he felt like an idiot for not saying it sooner.

"I should have told you earlier. Hell, I should have

told you a long time ago. But you'd made up your mind about Harold, and I thought it would be easier if you didn't know. I thought you didn't want to know."

She tugged him down onto the bed beside her. "So what changed your mind?"

"I thought you needed a choice—be with a man like Harold who can offer you the world, or be with a guy like me who can only offer you his love."

Her smile broadened and some of the tension eased from his body. "Well, that's a no-brainer." She squinted at him. "But is that a proposal, Mr. Moretti?"

"Yeah, it is," he said, realizing for the first time that there was no way he was leaving the island without Kyra at his side.

"Good," she said, twisting to kiss him. "Then that's a yes."

His heart swelled, and he took her hand, filled to the brim with love. But he also wanted her to understand what she would be giving up. "You know I can't help with your business."

"Yes, you can," she said, her eyes earnest. "It's going to be rough for a while. But don't you see? You help just by being there, just by holding my hand."

He did that then, closing his hand around her fingers and squeezing tight until she felt his warmth and strength fill her. "Always, sweetheart. That's a promise."

They fell into each other's arms, spooning together on the mattress, lost in a haze of love and happiness—

sentimental as hell, but it felt damn good. He took another deep breath, letting the truth sink deeper into his bones. She loved him. She really loved him.

In the months since the accident, he'd thought he had it so bad. He'd been a damn fool. He didn't have it hard, not at all. At least not anymore. He had Kyra. And that made him the luckiest man on the face of the earth.

"My brother will understand," she continued. "For that matter, I think Harold will, too. My dad will be harder, but I think he'll get used to it. His bottom line is for me to be happy, so even if he blusters for a while, he'll be fine. And as for me..." She shrugged. "Well, if I can go it alone and keep the business alive, great. But if not, I'm sure there's someone else out there willing to hire me."

He shook his head. "That won't work."

"Why not?" She turned her head to face him, her eyes wide, and he knew he wouldn't be able to tease her for long.

"Because I don't intend to ever let you go it alone."

"Yeah?" She snuggled even closer, and he pressed a kiss to the top of her head.

"Yeah."

"Promise?"

On his life. "I promise."

She shifted, rolling over in his arms and propping herself up on one elbow.

She slid her arms around his neck. "Thank you," she whispered.

"For what?"

"For everything. For being you." She snuggled closer. "For making me realize that I couldn't live my life based on a list of pros and cons. That I needed to live it for myself." She tilted her head back, brushed her lips over his. "With you," she whispered.

"I love you," he said, his heart swelling as he leaned in to press his mouth to hers.

She was really his—not Harold's—Tony's. She loved him, and she wanted to be with him. With a sigh, he pulled her closer, his fingers stroking her back. Somehow, despite everything, in the end, he really had managed to rescue the woman he loved.

And that, he thought, was a fantasy come true.

Epilogue

MERRILEE WATCHED as the plane rose off the water, her hand cupped over her forehead to block the sun. In the window, she could see Kyra and Tony waving goodbye, and she returned the gesture with a smile, watching until the plane was little more than a dot in the sky.

"What a great happily ever after for those two," Danielle said.

"Oh, yes. We couldn't have hoped for a better result." Tony had found a woman who loved him so fiercely it forced him to finally believe he was worthy of her love.

And Kyra...well, she'd had the chance to live what was fast becoming Merrilee's own personal fantasy—the mysterious stranger in her life and the man of her dreams had turned out to be one and the same.

As she and Danielle headed back to the main building, Merrilee fingered the heart-shaped ruby necklace she'd found that morning on her pillow. In so many ways, her admirer really did seem to know her secrets, and in those soft moments between sleep and dreams, she even allowed herself to pretend that the array of flowers and gifts were from her Charlie—that he was somewhere nearby, waiting to surprise her, waiting to fulfill the biggest fantasy of all.

But that, of course, was impossible. Her Charlie wasn't coming back, no matter how hard she wished for it. Soon, she'd find out who was leaving her gifts. Already he'd made her feel special, and she had no intention of waiting until he decided to show himself. It was time to take matters into her own hands.

Still, no matter how nice it was to have an admirer, the fantasy that he was Charlie lived in her dreams. She allowed herself one moment of melancholy, then put an arm around Danielle's shoulder and gave the girl a motherly squeeze.

"Come on. Let's get back to the office and review the most recent applications. It's time we helped make another fantasy come true."

* * * * *

The fantasy continues in

WILD FANTASY

by Janelle Denison
Available in August 2001

*Three sizzling love stories
by today's hottest writers
can be found in...*

Midnight Fantasies....

Feel the heat!

Available July 2001

MYSTERY LOVER—*Vicki Lewis Thompson*
When an unexpected storm hits, rancher Jonas Garfield
takes cover in a nearby cave...and finds himself seduced
senseless by an enigmatic temptress who refuses to tell him
her name. All he knows is that this sexy woman wants him.
And for Jonas, that's enough—for now....

AFTER HOURS—*Stephanie Bond*
Michael Pierce has always considered costume shop
owner Rebecca Valentine no more than an associate—
until he drops by her shop one night and witnesses the
mousy wallflower's transformation into a seductive siren.
Suddenly he's desperate to know her much better.
But which woman is the real Rebecca?

SHOW AND TELL—*Kimberly Raye*
A naughty lingerie party. A forbidden fantasy. When Texas
bad boy Dallas Jericho finds a slip of paper left over from
the party, he is surprised—and aroused—to discover that he
is good girl Laney Merriweather's wildest fantasy. So what
can he do but show the lady what she's been missing....

Fantasies Inc.

An exclusive agency that caters to intimate whims, provocative requests and decadent desires...

Four lush island resorts waiting to transport guests into a private world of sensual adventures, erotic pleasures and seductive passions...

A miniseries that will leave readers breathless and yearning for more...

Don't miss:
#832 SEDUCTIVE FANTASY by Janelle Denison
Available May 2001

#836 SECRET FANTASY by Carly Phillips
Available June 2001

#840 INTIMATE FANTASY by Julie Kenner
Available July 2001

#844 WILD FANTASY by Janelle Denison
Available August 2001

Do you have a secret fantasy?

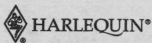

HARLEQUIN®

makes any time special—online...

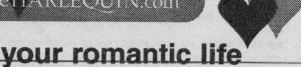

your romantic life

◆—Romance 101————
♥ Guides to romance, dating and flirting.

◆—Dr. Romance ————
♥ Get romance advice and tips from
our expert, Dr. Romance.

◆—Recipes for Romance——
♥ How to plan romantic meals for you
and your sweetie.

◆—Daily Love Dose————
♥ Tips on how to keep the romance
alive every day.

◆—Tales from the Heart———
♥ Discuss romantic dilemmas with other
members in our Tales from the Heart
message board.

HINTL1R

*Harlequin truly does
make any time special....
This year we are celebrating
weddings in style!*

A Walk Down the Aisle
WEDDING CELEBRATION

To help us celebrate, we want you to tell us how wearing the Harlequin wedding gown will make your wedding day special. As the grand prize, Harlequin will offer one lucky bride the chance to **"Walk Down the Aisle"** in the Harlequin wedding gown!

There's more...

For her honeymoon, she and her groom will spend five nights at the **Hyatt Regency Maui.** As part of this five-night honeymoon at the hotel renowned for its romantic attractions, the couple will enjoy a candlelit dinner for two in Swan Court, a sunset sail on the hotel's catamaran, and duet spa treatments.

A HYATT RESORT AND SPA

Maui • Molokai • Lanai

To enter, please write, in, 250 words or less, how wearing the Harlequin wedding gown will make your wedding day special. The entry will be judged based on its emotionally compelling nature, its originality and creativity, and its sincerity. This contest is open to Canadian and U.S. residents only and to those who are 18 years of age and older. There is no purchase necessary to enter. Void where prohibited. See further contest rules attached. Please send your entry to:

Walk Down the Aisle Contest

In Canada	In U.S.A.
P.O. Box 637	P.O. Box 9076
Fort Erie, Ontario	3010 Walden Ave.
L2A 5X3	Buffalo, NY 14269-9076

You can also enter by visiting www.eHarlequin.com
Win the Harlequin wedding gown and the vacation of a lifetime!
The deadline for entries is October 1, 2001.

HARLEQUIN®
Makes any time special ®

PHWDACONT1

1. To enter, follow directions published in the offer to which you are responding. Contest begins April 2, 2001, and ends on October 1, 2001. Method of entry may vary. Mailed entries must be postmarked by October 1, 2001, and received by October 8, 2001.

2. Contest entry may be, at times, presented via the Internet, but will be restricted solely to residents of certain geographic areas that are disclosed on the Web site. To enter via the Internet, if permissible, access the Harlequin Web site (www.eHarlequin.com) and follow the directions displayed online. Online entries must be received by 11:59 p.m. E.S.T. on October 1, 2001.

   In lieu of submitting an entry online, enter by mail by hand-printing (or typing) on an 8½" x 11" plain piece of paper, your name, address (including zip code), Contest number/name and in 250 words or fewer, why winning a Harlequin wedding dress would make your wedding day special. Mail via first-class mail to: Harlequin Walk Down the Aisle Contest 1197, (in the U.S.) P.O. Box 9076, 3010 Walden Avenue, Buffalo, NY 14269-9076, (in Canada) P.O. Box 637, Fort Erie, Ontario L2A 5X3, Canada.

   Limit one entry per person, household address and e-mail address. Online and/or mailed entries received from persons residing in geographic areas in which Internet entry is not permissible will be disqualified.

3. Contests will be judged by a panel of members of the Harlequin editorial, marketing and public relations staff based on the following criteria:
   - Originality and Creativity—50%
   - Emotionally Compelling—25%
   - Sincerity—25%

   In the event of a tie, duplicate prizes will be awarded. Decisions of the judges are final.

4. All entries become the property of Torstar Corp. and will not be returned. No responsibility is assumed for lost, late, illegible, incomplete, inaccurate, nondelivered or misdirected mail or misdirected e-mail, for technical, hardware or software failures of any kind, lost or unavailable network connections, or failed, incomplete, garbled or delayed computer transmission or any human error which may occur in the receipt or processing of the entries in this Contest.

5. Contest open only to residents of the U.S. (except Puerto Rico) and Canada, who are 18 years of age or older, and is void wherever prohibited by law; all applicable laws and regulations apply. Any litigation within the Province of Quebec respecting the conduct or organization of a publicity contest may be submitted to the Régie des alcools, des courses et des jeux for a ruling. Any litigation respecting the awarding of a prize may be submitted to the Régie des alcools, des courses et des jeux only for the purpose of helping the parties reach a settlement. Employees and immediate family members of Torstar Corp. and D. L. Blair, Inc., their affiliates, subsidiaries and all other agencies, entities and persons connected with the use, marketing or conduct of this Contest are not eligible to enter. Taxes on prizes are the sole responsibility of winners. Acceptance of any prize offered constitutes permission to use winner's name, photograph or other likeness for the purposes of advertising, trade and promotion on behalf of Torstar Corp., its affiliates and subsidiaries without further compensation to the winner, unless prohibited by law.

6. Winners will be determined no later than November 15, 2001, and will be notified by mail. Winners will be required to sign and return an Affidavit of Eligibility form within 15 days after winner notification. Noncompliance within that time period may result in disqualification and an alternative winner may be selected. Winners of trip must execute a Release of Liability prior to ticketing and must possess required travel documents (e.g. passport, photo ID) where applicable. Trip must be completed by November 2002. No substitution of prize permitted by winner. Torstar Corp. and D. L. Blair, Inc., their parents, affiliates, and subsidiaries are not responsible for errors in printing or electronic presentation of Contest, entries and/or game pieces. In the event of printing or other errors which may result in unintended prize values or duplication of prizes, all affected game pieces or entries shall be null and void. If for any reason the Internet portion of the Contest is not capable of running as planned, including infection by computer virus, bugs, tampering, unauthorized intervention, fraud, technical failures, or any other causes beyond the control of Torstar Corp. which corrupt or affect the administration, secrecy, fairness, integrity or proper conduct of the Contest, Torstar Corp. reserves the right, at its sole discretion, to disqualify any individual who tampers with the entry process and to cancel, terminate, modify or suspend the Contest or the Internet portion thereof. In the event of a dispute regarding an online entry, the entry will be deemed submitted by the authorized holder of the e-mail account submitted at the time of entry. Authorized account holder is defined as the natural person who is assigned to an e-mail address by an Internet access provider, online service provider or other organization that is responsible for arranging e-mail address for the domain associated with the submitted e-mail address. Purchase or acceptance of a product offer does not improve your chances of winning.

7. Prizes: (1) Grand Prize—A Harlequin wedding dress (approximate retail value: $3,500) and a 5-night/6-day honeymoon trip to Maui, HI, including round-trip air transportation provided by Maui Visitors Bureau from Los Angeles International Airport (winner is responsible for transportation to and from Los Angeles International Airport) and a Harlequin Romance Package, including hotel accomodations (double occupancy) at the Hyatt Regency Maui Resort and Spa, dinner for (2) two at Swan Court, a sunset sail on Kiele V and a spa treatment for the winner (approximate retail value: $4,000); (5) Five runner-up prizes of a $1000 gift certificate to selected retail outlets to be determined by Sponsor (retail value $1000 ea.). Prizes consist of only those items listed as part of the prize. Limit one prize per person. All prizes are valued in U.S. currency.

8. For a list of winners (available after December 17, 2001) send a self-addressed, stamped envelope to: Harlequin Walk Down the Aisle Contest 1197 Winners, P.O. Box 4200 Blair, NE 68009-4200 or you may access the www.eHarlequin.com Web site through January 15, 2002.

Contest sponsored by Torstar Corp., P.O. Box 9042, Buffalo, NY 14269-9042, U.S.A.

PHWDACONT2

Double your pleasure—
with this collection containing two full-length

Harlequin Romance®

novels

New York Times bestselling author

DEBBIE MACOMBER

delivers

RAINY DAY KISSES

While Susannah Simmons struggles up the corporate
ladder, her neighbor Nate Townsend stays home baking
cookies and flying kites. She resents the way he questions
her values—and the way he messes up her five-year plan
when she falls in love with him!

PLUS

THE BRIDE PRICE

a brand-new novel by reader favorite

DAY LECLAIRE

On sale July 2001

HARLEQUIN®

Makes any time special ®

Visit us at www.eHarlequin.com

PHROM